The Desert Eagle's booming roar filled the air

Bolan took down the two men who tried to rush his position. That left two, both of whom had taken cover on the far side of his truck, shooting wildly. Panic was a wonderful field tool.

He opened up once more, hitting each man in the lower leg. The powerful weapon all but tore limbs off at this range. He worked his way around to the far side of the truck and finished the job.

Bolan scanned the area and saw nothing but bodies. On the ground near one of them, he spotted the radio and could hear his enemy demanding information.

He picked it up and keyed the mike. "That's just the beginning," he told the man. "I'll see you and Sureno real soon." He threw the radio to the ground and moved toward the nearby group of vehicles, hoping to find some supplies for his trek across the desert.

Perhaps he was tired, or perhaps he was simply too focused on his search. Either way, Bolan didn't see the man who'd taken shelter in the backseat of the first car he approached until he lunged forward, gun in hand.

MACK BOLAN ®
The Executioner

The Don Pendleton's
Executioner®
DESERT IMPACT

A GOLD EAGLE BOOK FROM
W🌐RLDWIDE®

TORONTO • NEW YORK • LONDON
AMSTERDAM • PARIS • SYDNEY • HAMBURG
STOCKHOLM • ATHENS • TOKYO • MILAN
MADRID • WARSAW • BUDAPEST • AUCKLAND

Recycling programs
for this product may
not exist in your area.

First edition July 2014

ISBN-13: 978-0-373-64428-5

Special thanks and acknowledgment to
Dylan Garrett for his contribution to this work.

DESERT IMPACT

Printed in U.S.A.

Fast is fine, but accuracy is final.
—Wyatt Earp

I'm not interested in speed for its own sake. But I will do what it takes to catch up with those who would try to outrun their own judgment.
—Mack Bolan

THE
MACK BOLAN
LEGEND

Nothing less than a war could have fashioned the destiny of the man called Mack Bolan. Bolan earned the Executioner title in the jungle hell of Vietnam.

But this soldier also wore another name—Sergeant Mercy. He was so tagged because of the compassion he showed to wounded comrades-in-arms and Vietnamese civilians.

Mack Bolan's second tour of duty ended prematurely when he was given emergency leave to return home and bury his family, victims of the Mob. Then he declared a one-man war against the Mafia.

He confronted the Families head-on from coast to coast, and soon a hope of victory began to appear. But Bolan had broken society's every rule. That same society started gunning for this elusive warrior—to no avail.

So Bolan was offered amnesty to work within the system against terrorism. This time, as an employee of Uncle Sam, Bolan became Colonel John Phoenix. With a command center at Stony Man Farm in Virginia, he and his new allies—Able Team and Phoenix Force—waged relentless war on a new adversary: the KGB.

But when his one true love, April Rose, died at the hands of the Soviet terror machine, Bolan severed all ties with Establishment authority.

Now, after a lengthy lone-wolf struggle and much soul-searching, the Executioner has agreed to enter an "arm's-length" alliance with his government once more, reserving the right to pursue personal missions in his Everlasting War.

1

The borderlands were nothing more than long stretches of desert, patches of sage and prickly mesquite trees. Old wooden fences and faded barbwire strands, and from time to time, a decent fence that some desperate rancher put up only to have it torn down by the illegals crossing everywhere but at the actual checkpoints. During the heat of the day, the sun glanced off hills and rocks, filling the arid land with shimmering illusions in the rippling heat. But the night…the night was altogether different. Under a full moon, the desert became a luminescent landscape filled with creatures on the hunt, no longer pinned down by the oppressive heat. Shadows pooled beneath rocky outcroppings and the hunting cries of owls echoed in the wind.

Colton Rivers, a field operations supervisor for the United States Border Patrol, stared out at the desert night, waiting to see if the intelligence they'd obtained was accurate. From California to Texas, some portions of the border were more porous than others. The Arizona border was Swiss cheese. He was based in Douglas, right across from Agua Prieta, Mexico, and every year the situation got worse. There was no explaining to the politicians that it wasn't the number of officers that mattered, but the fact that a night in one of their cells was still a trip to heaven for many of the people who crossed over. Mexico was all but an undeclared war zone, and the drug lords were running most of the countryside. Sadly, fewer and fewer families were actually crossing the border in search of a better life—many families were just trying to get away. Other immigrants were drug and weapon runners—mules—and the thugs who transported people into the United States for outrageous fees.

The working life of a Border Patrol agent was getting more dangerous, too. Fewer men and women were willing to take the risks, in spite of decent pay and benefits, and of those who did, many were injured or killed every year. It wasn't an easy job, and it was often damn thankless, but Rivers was proud to be doing it. Every time they made an arrest, it was one small step toward making the border more secure. Still, it was only a matter of time until the flood waters overwhelmed them, or worse, some terrorist found a way through the desert and into the United States with a dirty bomb. Rivers shook his head, bringing his mind back to the night's mission.

A runner arrested two days before had told them that a large arms shipment was coming in, but Rivers was having a hell of a time believing that was the case. The full moon was practically a spotlight. A large vehicle would be far too easy to spot moving across the barren landscape.

"What do you think?" the man standing next to him asked. His name was Craig Jennings, and he was so fresh from the academy that the shine still hadn't worn off his badge—or his face. He was surveying the desert floor through a pair of night vision goggles, a bundle of nervous energy. At thirty, Rivers felt like the old man of the group and was not as prone to get excited with every tip they were given. Too often, leads were nothing more than dead ends or even purposeful misinformation. The drug and weapon dealers on the other side of the border were many things, but the successful ones were far from stupid.

Rivers scanned the empty desert once more, and then shook his head. "I think we've been out here for over an hour and haven't seen shit. Even if it was going to happen, they probably called it off on account of the moon."

"Pack up?" Craig asked.

He nodded. "Yeah, let's pack it in for the night. This was overtime duty for all of us anyway. If we get our asses back to the station, we might actually get a few hours of sleep before the next shift. It might be nice to see my little girl, if she can remember what her dad looks like."

Rivers smiled at Jennings's crestfallen expression, but he really was ready to go home and see his family, and he knew the rest of his team was too. His squad was the best trained in the area and people vied for a position on it, but with the training came the hours, and with each passing day the hours felt longer. Field work was really best left to men without families—or social lives. Probably should include it in the official job description, he thought morosely as Jennings jumped down from the Ford Expedition's running boards.

Rivers lifted his binoculars for one last look. Just as he was ready to end the operation, he saw a faint gleam of light at the edge of a distant sand hill, only to watch it disappear. A flicker and it was gone.

"Hold on…" he said, looking again. Nothing. "Give me your night vision, Jennings."

Jennings handed over the goggles. Rivers didn't bother slipping the straps over his head, just held them up to his eyes and adjusted the distance. Other than a few small heat signatures from random desert creatures, the landscape still looked quiet. He knew that in these situations, patience was a field agent's best friend, so he focused in on the hill where the light had briefly flickered and waited.

Beside him, Jennings started to speak, but Rivers shushed him and continued to watch. Finally, along the base of the mound, people began to appear, followed by a large truck. How the hell they'd gotten it *into* the hill was a mystery for later. Right now, the primary goal needed to be an arrest. "Hold on, guys," Rivers said after keying his mike. "We've got company."

Over several minutes, five trucks lined up, and more were emerging. The tunnel must have been huge and taken months to build. Headlights were now clearly visible. "Everyone stand by," Rivers added, continuing to watch the developing scene. This was a big group, sure, but they were brazen as hell.

"What's that?" Jennings asked, as the sound of heavy engines filled the air.

From a space somewhere between the squad's position and where the illegals were gathering, two massive spotlights burst to life. Rivers yanked the goggles away from his eyes but not before he was half-blinded. He blinked rapidly to clear his vision and almost panicked as two modified assault vehicles—ultralight and modeled after rock-crawling dune buggies—came tearing toward them. Rivers caught a quick glimpse of mounted guns a second or two before they opened fire.

The unforgettable sound of two .50 caliber machine

guns cut through the night. "Get down!" Rivers yelled, jumping free from the Expedition as bullets pierced the armored vehicle and strafed the ground.

His men ran for cover as Rivers rolled, got to his feet and spun back to jump behind the wheel of the truck. He turned the motor over and threw the truck into gear. After serving four years in the Army Special Forces and nearly eight years in the field as a Border Patrol agent, he knew the illegals' expectation would be that they'd run like hell. He punched the accelerator and drove straight at the nearest buggy, even as rounds from the machine gun chewed holes in his hood. He yanked his Glock 17 free from the holster and began blasting through the window as he careened sideways.

Rivers's charge forced the buggy to turn, but that didn't stop the other one from taking its own shots at him. Rivers spun the wheel, and the Expedition's tires clawed for traction. He nearly rolled the truck before it slammed back onto the rocky ground. Jennings had somehow made it into the vehicle, but all he could do was hold on. His face was white as a sheet.

"Either get your ass down, or do something," Rivers snarled, wishing that spots on his team could be limited to men with at least a few years of field experience.

The new recruit grabbed the dash and ducked onto the floor as the second dune buggy closed in on them. Rivers dropped the transmission into reverse and slammed on the gas. The assault vehicle tried to adjust but hit a rock outcropping and flipped over twice before landing on its wheels and coming after them again. Hitting the brakes, Rivers jammed the transmission back into drive, then floored it, ramming the buggy at full speed. Men screamed as the two vehicles crunched together with the sound of tearing metal. One man flew forward and smashed into his windshield, leaving a smear of blood and brains on the bulletproof glass before sliding off the hood. With that buggy finally finished off, Rivers backed up and turned around, heading for where his other men were holed up.

He could see two agents on the ground by their vehicles. A jeep had joined the other dune buggy and had the remaining agents pinned down. Rivers swerved to hit a berm, which launched the Expedition into the fray and gave the agents cover. Gunfire from the automatic weapons on the dune buggy and the jeep knocked out two of the Expedition's tires, dropping the hulking three tons of steel into the desert sand and throwing him into the windshield.

A sharp spike of pain lanced through his skull as his nose broke and the skin of his forehead split on impact. He leaned back, wiping the blood out of his eyes with a pained grunt.

"Are we going to die?" Jennings asked from the floor.

"If we just sit here, we will," he replied. "It's move or die time."

Rivers reached into the backseat, the armor on the modified truck giving them at least a couple of moments before they'd be completely overwhelmed, and opened the lid for more weapons. He pulled out three grenades, giving one to Jennings, who was trying to pull himself together. Rivers tucked the other two grenades in his belt, then grabbed an FN SCAR assault rifle and two extra clips.

He'd been given the weapon to field test it and he sure hoped it proved to be reliable. Rivers popped two smoke grenades and chucked them out the window for cover, then burst out of the vehicle's passenger side with Jennings close on his heels. They worked their way along the side of the Expedition, joining the two agents that had been pinned down behind a cluster of boulders.

Rivers heard Jennings yelp and turned back, his Glock 17 in his hand. Jennings looked terrified as his captor wrenched his head backward.

"Drop it," the man said.

"I don't think so," Rivers replied.

The shot from the Glock was smooth and the look of surprise was etched on the captor's face for a small moment before the bullet in his skull killed the lights. Rivers barely broke stride as he grabbed Jennings and pulled him in his wake.

It looked like the illegals were assessing the situation, so Rivers took advantage of the delay and lobbed one grenade into the dune buggy and the second into the jeep. The explosions lit up the night—and the two vehicles—ensuring that, at least for the moment, everyone was on foot. The thugs who had been pressing closer ran for cover.

"Rivers," one of the other agents said after the echoes faded away. "I called for support before it all went to hell, but I don't know how long it will take to get here."

As if on cue, they heard a helicopter making its way toward them. Rivers popped a flare from his vest, the trailing orange smoke showing the agents' location. The gunship moved in for a strafing run, giving the agents time to fall back to one of the other vehicles. They piled inside as the chopper moved in sweeping patterns, keeping them safe. The rest of their assailants moved back into the desert, disappearing almost as quickly as they'd appeared.

The chopper landed and Rivers moved back in for a closer look. The paperwork on this would be tremendous, and he was still very uncertain how the hell they ended up in this mess in the first place. Where had the illegals all come from, and how had they gotten their hands on those kinds of weapons and vehicles?

He walked over to one of the wrecked dune buggies. There would be no questioning the mangled bodies that littered the area. He ran his flashlight beam across the wreckage, then paused as he came upon the .50 caliber machine gun. It was a Browning all right and carried U.S. Army serial numbers and badging. He ran his hands along the raised lettering.

"Son of a bitch," he muttered. "I don't believe it."

"What is it?" Jennings asked.

Rivers ran his light across the letters again. He nodded at Jennings's indrawn breath.

"Those are Army weapons," Jennings said. "Now what do we do?"

"Now we get some help," Rivers replied. "Because if this means what I think it does, we're going to need it."

2

From the top of Holtanna Peak in Antarctica, Mack Bolan took a deep, cleansing breath. The landscape was pure, white snow, broken only by jagged shards of brown rock. Here, there were no human enemies to fight, no wars to win. The cold, the wind, the challenges of climbing, skiing and BASE jumping in this region were daunting, but for a man known as the Executioner, this kind of activity was his idea of rest and relaxation.

The tall pillar of Holtanna topped out at almost nine thousand feet. Standing alone in the middle of the Antarctic, the "hollow tooth" was an obstacle meant to be conquered. Bolan and his climbing companion, Gerard Casias, led the way, setting ropes for the other two climbers. Even with his winter gear, the cold penetrated deep into his bones. Each time he pushed in with the ice spikes on the soles of his boots, sharp pins of pain radiated through his frozen skin and up his leg. He wiggled his toes to increase the circulation before he looked for his next foothold. The chimneys within the rock were choked with snow, making the climb slow and arduous. Bolan paused to look out over the pristine white landscape. The sheer beauty of the environment pushed him onward. He placed the next piton to hold the permanent rope for the rest of the crew to climb behind him.

At two a.m. in Antarctica, the sun was high, but the temperature was not. The light beard Bolan had grown to help protect his face was frozen. The trek had taken them twenty-four hours of straight climbing.

Standing now on top of the bottom of the world, Bolan saw an incoming aircraft and pulled out his field goggles to identify it. A P3-K Orion, which meant that his time off was about to be cut short. Someone was using U.S. Naval resources to find him.

He took one last look at the beautiful surroundings, then zipped the last of the closures on his wingsuit. The material created the illusion of wings and a tail.

"Who will count it off?" Gerard called out.

"I will," Bolan said.

He waited by the ledge, took two strides and launched himself into the abyss. The wind rushed past him, but the edges of his suit broke the speed and created a nice glide through the air. Bolan experimented with the directions of his arms and the angle of his body as he played on the breeze. Closing in on his mark, he deployed the parachute and glided safely to the ground. The others were right behind him. He unclipped the parachute, waved to the other climbers and sprinted off toward the plane as it taxied to a halt.

Gerard would see to it that the others got back to camp and would most likely stay for another few weeks, enjoying a life of adventure that didn't involve the kinds of dangers the Executioner faced most every day of his life.

The cabin door opened on the aircraft and a ladder was tossed through the opening. Bolan stopped and looked up to see a grizzled E-7 staring down at him. "Colonel Stone?" the man shouted, trying to make himself heard over the props.

"That's me," Bolan yelled. "You must be my ride."

"Yes, sir! We've got orders to get you back to the States as fast as possible."

Bolan started climbing the ladder, and after a couple of minutes, he stepped on board. The chief petty officer gave him a quick once over. "You don't look like a colonel," he quipped.

"I've been off-duty," Bolan replied. "Let's get moving."

"Yes, sir," the man said, pulling in the ladder and slamming the cabin door shut.

Bolan moved to the cockpit and opened the door. Two officers—the pilot and the copilot—were inside. "Gentlemen," he said.

"Colonel Stone," the pilot said. "I'm Captain Sikes, and this is Lieutenant Commander Olsen. Glad we were able to find you so quickly. We've got orders."

"I figured as much," Bolan replied. "What's our route back?"

"We'll go via South America," Sikes said. "We'll take on a new crew there, and then get you home."

"Sounds like a long, boring flight," he said.

"That's just how we like them, sir," Olsen replied.

"Go ahead and make yourself comfortable in back," Sikes added.

Bolan nodded and headed to the cabin, where he found the other man already seated in the front row. He stopped in the galley long enough to grab some hot coffee, then moved to the back of the cabin and took a seat. The props began to spin faster and the plane completed a long turn, then started down the rough landing strip before heading into the sky.

From his inside jacket pocket, Bolan pulled out his handheld and powered it up. It took a good minute for it to sync with the satellite system it used for communications. As soon as he had a good signal, he put his thumb on the screen and unlocked the device. He opened his contacts and hit a speed-dial number. It took several seconds for the call to connect but only one ring before Hal Brognola, the director of the Sensitive Operations Group, based at Stony Man Farm, to answer.

"Tell me you're on the plane, Striker," he said, skipping any formalities.

"I'm on the plane," he assured him.

"We've got a situation and I need you in on it."

Stony Man Farm was a clandestine organization whose action teams fought terrorism and crime all over the world. When the mission was such that official agencies couldn't openly take it on, Stony Man stepped in, thus allowing the U.S. Government to disavow involvement. Bolan worked with the Farm at arm's length, taking on missions when it was crucial or appropriate and bringing in new missions when he needed backup in terms of technology, weapons and sometimes manpower. For Brognola to have back-channeled him into a Navy plane using his Colonel Stone identity, the situation must be pretty dire.

"What's the problem, Hal?" he asked.

"Well, the good news is that you're going somewhere warmer."

"Anywhere is warmer than here," Bolan said.

"True enough," he admitted. "The situation is this— one of our field assets in Phoenix got in touch with us two days ago. She was contacted by a U.S. Border Patrol agent named Colton Rivers."

"Hmm…there's a name I haven't heard in a while," Bolan said. "He's one of their field ops guys on the border. We crossed paths a while back when I dealt with that rash of agent kidnappings."

"Same guy," Brognola said. "He didn't know how to find you, so he asked around and eventually connected with me."

"So, what's going on that Rivers thinks he needs help from people like us?"

"The smuggling situation down there has taken a turn for the surreal. He was out with a team in the desert near Douglas and they were ambushed by illegals from the other side."

"That's probably not all that unusual," Bolan replied. "It's a war zone, Hal. A quiet one, but still war."

"If that were all, I wouldn't be talking to you. There's more. The weapons the illegals were using were U.S. Army issue. Not surplus, either. Someone is selling them military weapons, and if it's hot down there now, a cartel armed with God-knows-what could turn that quiet war-zone into a full-scale disaster area."

"That's attention-getting, all right. Does this have anything to do with the whole Fast and Furious mess the ATF created? If so, isn't it the government's problem?"

"I don't think so," Brognola said. "Most of that has been cleaned up, and those were small weapons. These are .50 caliber machine guns, mounted on all-terrain dune buggies. The men were armed with standard-issue assault rifles, too."

Bolan whistled. That was heavy hardware. "Okay,"

he said. "I'll call Rivers now if you can forward me his number. Where am I landing in the U.S.?"

"Phoenix, by way of Dallas," Brognola replied. "According to our Naval contacts, you'll be on the ground in Arizona in less than twenty-four hours."

"All right," Bolan said. "I'll need a vehicle and a basic field set—you know what I need."

"It will be waiting for you at the airport. Do you want me to organize backup for you? I can hook you up with a Phoenix-based agent, Nadia Merice."

Bolan considered it for a moment. "Not just yet," he said. "Send me her dossier and contact information. Let me go down and assess the situation first. If I need her, I'll get in touch."

"You'll have all of it shortly, Striker. Keep me informed, please. We don't want this spiraling out of control."

"Will do," Bolan said, then hung up the phone. A few moments later, the number for Colton River came through as a secured text message. He dialed it.

"Rivers," the vaguely familiar voice answered.

"Agent Rivers, Matt Cooper," he said. "I heard you were trying to find me."

"Cooper! I didn't think I'd be able to track you down. Not really."

"It's a small world," Bolan said. "What can I do for you?"

Colton quickly explained his situation, and it lined up with what Brognola had told him. "I know you're not... well, official, but I think that's just what we need. Especially if official people are involved."

Bolan lay back in his seat and listened, rolling the information over in his head. Rivers was a good man, and he was obviously in a bit of a panic. He'd stopped talking, but Bolan was unwilling to speak for the moment. The silence made the agent nervous.

"Cooper, are you still there?"

"Yeah, I'm here," he said, staring out the window. Below, the edge of the ice was giving way to the choppy waters of the Southern Ocean.

"Thank you, Cooper. I didn't know who else could handle this kind of thing."

"It sounds sticky. We'll talk more when I get there," he said, then disconnected the call. Brognola was right about at least one thing, he thought—he was going somewhere warmer.

3

The contrast between the stark, icy white of the Antarctic and the brash gold and tan of the desert had been more than a little startling. After a long flight into Phoenix, Bolan had picked up a car and driven east, passing through Tucson, then cutting south through Sierra Vista and finally arriving in Douglas, Arizona. The dry desert winds blew tumbleweeds across the highway as Bolan drove into the outskirts of the small town.

It was a bit eerie—a town with main streets that hadn't seen much in the way of updating since the seventies. The only modern storefronts he saw were those of a Wal-Mart and a McDonald's, which he passed without slowing. Douglas was positioned directly on the border with Mexico, and the flow of immigrants—both legal and illegal—was enough to make Caucasian people a minority. On the other side of the border was Agua Prieta, a much larger city, with much bigger problems. Drug trafficking and illegal immigrants were big business in Agua Prieta, and many honest cops on that side were killed with disturbing regularity.

Bolan pulled up to the gas station where he was meeting Rivers and waved off the entrepreneurs selling fresh tamales out of the trunk of their car. Bolan didn't try to hide the fact that he was carrying, and he kept a wary eye on those milling about. Enough crime occurred in this one little corner of the universe to keep county, state and federal law enforcement busy every day of the year. It wouldn't do to become a statistic.

Bolan continued to eye the comings and goings when a car pulled up to one of the pumps. The music was blaring loud enough that the bass thrummed through the gas station until the car shut down. Three guys in white tank tops stepped out of the souped-up Malibu from the eighties that looked like it was halfway through its restoration. One guy went into the gas station while the other two lagged behind and went to the old lady selling tamales.

"Hey, grandma, we could use some food."

"Five dollars for five."

"No, grandma, we just want the food."

They moved forward and Bolan felt like he was watching a bad movie as the two men approached her. Their harassment of the old lady wasn't entertaining at all.

Bolan approached and tapped the closer of the two on the shoulder.

"What do you want?" he asked Bolan.

"You're going to leave this lady alone."

He lifted the edge of his T-shirt to reveal the .38 he was carrying in his waistband.

"I think I do what I want."

"Oh, well, you should have said that from the beginning."

The thug started to turn when Bolan caught his shoulder and spun him around, using the added momentum to drive his fist into the man's face, shattering his nose and dropping him to his knees. Bolan whipped the Desert Eagle out of his holster and trained it on the other man before either of them knew what had happened.

"Now, explain to me what it is you want to do. After all, we decided that you get to do what you want. I just thought there should be a little more discussion on what that might be."

"I'll leave, I'll leave."

Bolan nodded as they scurried to their car. When the third man came back outside, they peeled out of the gas station and sped down the road. He turned to look at the old woman, who reached into her bag and handed him a tamale.

"Gracias."

"De nada."

Bolan leaned against his car and munched on his tamale. He didn't have to wait long for Rivers to pull up in his SUV. The people who'd been milling around recognized the Border Patrol agent and found better things to do with their time. Rivers pulled his tall frame out of the SUV and offered a strong handshake. "Cooper," he said, a thin smile crossing his face. "Thanks for coming so fast."

Returning the handshake, Bolan nodded. "No problem. I could use a little sunshine, and I'm happy to help any way that I can."

"Good," he said. "Why don't we drop off your car at the station? No one will bother it there, and then we can take a little ride."

Bolan agreed, got back into his rental and followed Rivers to the local Border Patrol station. It was a lot larger than many other stations, due in part to the amount of illegal immigrants they had to deal with and to the on-site holding facility. They passed through a heavy security gate, and Bolan parked his car while Rivers picked up a pass from the guard shack and stuck it on his windshield.

After signing back out, they headed north out of Douglas, and Bolan glanced at the man he'd helped before, his gaze asking an unspoken question.

"I have a friend I want you to meet," Rivers said. "He's a retired freelancer. Did undercover work for the U.S. Marshals, tracking for the Border Patrol, and if some of the rumors are true, he started his career in the Drug Enforcement Administration. Anyway, he's been out here forever, knows every nook and cranny between Douglas and Sierra Vista. He also knows all of the local bad guys. All of which make him very useful."

"Local bad guys?" Bolan asked.

"This part of the world attracts a lot of different types—and one of them is the person looking to disappear. If the Old West still exists anywhere, it's right here, Cooper. A lot of black hats live in single-wide trailers or old camp shacks and have a record as long as your arm—or longer."

"What a charming place," Bolan replied.

"It's not that bad," Colton said. "Plenty of good people are here, too. Lot of folks who just want to live their lives in peace."

Bolan nodded and watched as the desert landscape slipped past his window. The small highway carved a path between small mountain ranges.

A couple of miles before the border with New Mexico, Rivers turned off the highway and onto a dirt road that resembled a dried-out creek bed.

"How far out does this guy live?"

"We're almost there now. He likes to keep to himself. Has this thing about wanting to see people coming."

"Well, I get that. I'm just not sure moving to a remote desert is the answer."

"I don't know—after all the things you've seen and done, don't the peace and serenity sound good?"

"It sounds good, but even when I'm on the other side of the world they seem to track me down."

The desert was open around them, and in the distance Bolan could see free-range cattle and some of those trailers Rivers had mentioned. The road itself was filled with divots and holes, rocks, cow pies and at least one turtle basking in the late afternoon sun.

"Tell me more about this man we're meeting," Bolan said. "How long have you known him?"

"Most of my life," Rivers replied. "I grew up in Sierra Vista and Tony and my father worked together. He was to be my godfather, but he didn't think it was appropriate considering his line of work."

"Makes sense," Bolan said. "That kind of life doesn't lend itself to long life expectancies."

"Yeah."

"I see why he's a resource. He lived long enough to retire, and that's saying something."

They pulled into the driveway. Rivers slowed as guinea hens scattered in front of the SUV. The double-wide trailer had been modified with a screened-in porch, and large portions of the property were fenced and cross-fenced for the livestock.

Tony, a stout, silver-haired man, stepped out of the trailer, a woman perhaps ten years younger at his side. The two of them waved.

"That's his wife, Eleanor," Rivers said. "I hope you

didn't eat much today because she'll insist on feeding you and be insulted if you don't put away enough for two."

"Is the food any good?" Bolan asked.

"Worth the drive."

"Then I'm sure I'll manage just fine."

The SUV rolled to a stop and they both climbed out as Tony stepped forward and opened the gate that marked the edge of the small yard around their property. Two dogs, mixed-breed Labs of some kind, barked wildly and Tony snapped at them in Spanish, waving them away.

"Colton," he said, a broad grin lighting up his face. "Welcome, as always. I see you brought a friend."

The older man stepped forward, his left hand on his thigh supporting a small limp, but he didn't falter as he shook hands. His eyes assessed Bolan quickly, and the smile that had lit his face a moment before faded a bit. "A dangerous friend, I think."

"You're a fast study," Bolan said, extending a hand. "Matt Cooper."

Rivers started to speak, but Tony held up a hand to silence him. "Okay, Matt, though I'm not sure the name fits quite right. If Colton says you're okay, then I can believe that, but before you come in, we need to have an understanding."

Bolan kept his silence, waiting.

"I know a man," Tony continued. "He does mercenary work of one kind or another in parts of the world with names I can't pronounce and most of which I've never heard of. You know the type?"

"Yeah," Bolan said. "I do."

"I figured you would," he replied. "Anyway, this man is the nicest guy you would ever want to meet. He's a good man to share a meal with and a better man to share a drink with. I like him a lot."

"I'm not sure I get your point."

"My point," Tony said, "is two things. First, that man I was telling you about? He's also the most dangerous sonofabitch I know. When it comes to killing, something I guess we both know a little about, there's maybe no one who does it better."

"Tony," Rivers began. "Maybe we should…"

"Second," the old man continued, "is that you remind me a bit of him. Actually more than a bit. So you'll understand when I tell you that if you bring trouble to my door, that man I told you about, well, he owes me a favor, and I suspect he'd take it as no hardship to bring trouble to yours, Matt—or whatever your real name is." He crossed his arms as he finished and stared hard at Bolan.

Bolan felt a grin tugging at the corner of his lips, tried to stop it and then gave up. The old man hadn't lived an easy life, but his eyes were still damn sharp. Most likely, the threat was an empty one, but when a man reached a certain age, it was the only kind of threat he could really make. "I like you, Tony," he said. "You've got enough brass for any three men on your own, and now you've threatened me with sure death if I come bringing trouble. I don't. Matt may not be a perfect fit, but it seems to work out okay. I won't bring trouble to you, old timer. On that, you have my word."

Tony stared at him a minute more, then smiled and stuck out a hand. "Done and done," he said. "Come on up to the house. Eleanor will want to feed you both, I imagine."

The woman had waited on the porch, watching the exchange with interest, but now she stepped over to greet them. Bolan offered his hand but was pulled into a short, friendly embrace. Into his ear, she whispered, "Thank you for understanding," then pulled away again, giving Rivers a hug, too. She smelled like baking apples and corn bread and all the wonderful scents of home, but as they entered the trailer, he noted pictures on the wall of her riding horses and any number of trophies to go with them. She was just as extraordinary as her husband.

"Now you boys get in here, but leave all those guns by the door."

Rivers was already removing his weapons, and Bolan glanced at Tony.

"Don't worry, son. There's nothing to fear here. I have a suspicion that if you wanted it bad enough, you could get it quickly sitting here by the door."

Bolan pulled the Desert Eagle from the holster and placed it on the table next to the door. He was halfway across the room before Eleanor stopped him.

"You must be as forgetful as Tony," she scolded, "but you have an excuse. You don't know that I won't serve an armed man at my table. You can leave the ankle gun over there, too."

Rivers and Tony both smiled as they followed Eleanor and left Bolan to pull the small pistol tucked into his ankle holster and place it on the table next to the Desert Eagle.

"Now, you boys sit down and I'll fix you up something nice while you talk."

Bolan began to argue, but Rivers shook his head, dissuading him. Bolan took his seat at the table.

Once they were all seated, Tony leaned back in his chair and cocked an eyebrow at Rivers. "So, what brings you, Colton? We love it when you visit, but I'm pretty sure you didn't bring Mister…Cooper here without a reason."

"True enough," he said. "I figured you might have a bead on a situation we ran into a couple of days ago."

Rivers ran through the fight on the border, showing them photos on his phone of the weapons and the serial nomenclature. Tony nodded a few times but didn't interrupt until the younger man was finished, ending the story with his call to Bolan. Tony stared at Bolan and then looked at Rivers again. "This hasn't been in the papers or on the news," he said thoughtfully.

"We've managed to keep it quiet so far," Rivers replied. "But I don't think we can keep a lid on it forever—and it will blow sky high if it happens again."

Tony nodded, turning to Bolan. "What do you think of all of this?"

"The border's been a mess for years, and it's getting worse. Without evidence, I can't be sure of anything."

"You know, I ran this area for a long time. Nothing came in our out of here without me knowing. Some things we let by to keep the peace and some we laid down the law on. I've worked undercover for the worst thugs and then tracked them across half a continent to bring them to justice. I've learned to trust my gut, and it tells me your suspicions may be as good as most people's facts, so please, share them with us."

Bolan leaned back and pondered the man before him. Few people Bolan met in his life he felt he could trust, but there was something about this man that said he might just make the list. That was a very rare thing in his world.

"Normally, I'd say Mexican Mafia, maybe. They're a little more organized than most of the drug lords. Still, taking on U.S. military weapons is a little out of their league. On the other hand, with things heating up down here the way they have been, I wouldn't cross anything off of the list."

"Ten years ago, maybe even five, I would agree with you," Tony said. "But as you say, the border here is worse than it has ever been. Mexico can't keep a handle on any of their cartels and small paramilitary groups are all vying for power. The government is powerless, and they're basically fighting a civil war with about a dozen different factions wanting a place at the table. We can find out who is responsible on the other side of the border, but the selling of U.S. arms on this side is more concerning."

"We're going to poke around in Sierra Vista next," Bolan said. "A lot goes on at Fort We Gotcha that happens behind the scenes."

Tony and Rivers both nodded, apparently amused that Bolan knew the more colloquial name for Fort Huachuca.

"In the meantime," Tony said, "I'll make a little noise and see who I can roust from their dens south of the border. You boys be careful, though. Something about this feels downright dangerous."

"I'm always careful," Bolan said. "It's a habit."

"Not too careful to eat, I hope," Eleanor said, setting a plate piled high with tortillas on the table. "That's enough business talk. Eat first, solve problems after." The smells from the kitchen were mouthwatering and all three men dug into the meal with gusto. Sometimes, a good meal before battle was all a man could hope for.

4

Fort Huachuca was situated just outside the small town of Sierra Vista and was home to the U.S. Army Intelligence Center as well as the 9th Army Signal Command, among other electronic communications and intelligence-driven units.

The gate guard took one look at Bolan's identification, offered a quick, casual salute and sent him on his way. He'd offered the credentials that would get him access to damn near every military installation he could want: Colonel Brandon Stone.

In the distance, past the manicured lawns of the buildings closest to the heart of the fort, Bolan could see the yellow hangars of Libby Airfield, which was used by both military and civilian aircraft.

The building Bolan was looking for wasn't hard to find—a quick internet search on his handheld revealed that a civilian company, Kruegor Enterprises, was in charge of the weapon warehousing and storage facilities on the base. Although Kruegor couldn't actually hand the weapons out, they provided the building maintenance, basic security and administrative personnel, while the armory itself was manned by Army regulars.

Bolan found the main administrative office quite easily. He parked his vehicle, then decided to try something. Instead of entering through the main office doors, he strolled around to the side of the building, where a set of bay doors, large enough for trucks to pass through, were wide open. He entered, whistling to himself. At the moment, no vehicles parked were inside, and other than a bored-looking sergeant at a checkout desk, no one was around. A quick visual inspection showed no weapons in the main area, but a sign on the door behind the sergeant indicated that only authorized military personnel were allowed beyond that point.

Bolan gave a friendly wave to the man and flashed his credentials. When the sergeant waved him through, he continued into the main office. There, another man was bent over a file cabinet, oblivious to Bolan's presence and muttering to himself about the nuisance of inspections. The man's white shirt wasn't quite tucked in on the sides, where it was a little small, and small trickles of sweat had formed on his bald head. He gave the impression of a man who knew a lot more about paperwork than building security.

Bolan pulled the door shut behind him, rocking the picture on the wall, as the man wrenched up from his hunched position. "Jesus, you scared the hell out of me!" he exclaimed.

Bolan didn't say anything but eyed the thin wad of papers the man was tucking behind his back.

"Can I help you? I mean…what are you doing here? This is a restricted area."

"Yeah, I got that from the mountains of security," Bolan quipped.

"Everything that needs to be secured is, but that's none of your business anyway. What do you want?"

"That remains to be seen. Either way, I'm looking for Brett Kingston."

"He's out of the office right now."

"I'll wait," he said. "I'm patient."

"I don't know when he'll be back."

The main office door opened and a tall man strode inside. Bolan instantly recognized him as Kingston from the personnel file he'd studied earlier. Although he appeared closer to fifty than twenty, he was in excellent shape beneath his black polo and khaki slacks. An Airborne tattoo, along with the insignia from the 7th Special Forces group stood out on his bulging bicep. Bolan took a casual step back, folding his arms. It wouldn't do to underestimate a man who'd spent time training in guerilla warfare.

The man didn't seem to notice him right away, snapping, "Hansen, where the hell is that file I need?"

Hansen pulled the papers out from behind his back, clutching them to his chest for a moment before shoving them toward Kingston like they were about to burst into flames. Kingston took them, nodding, then turned his attention to Bolan. A small tic in his face registered how happy he was to see a stranger in his facilities.

"Who're you, then?"

"Colonel Brandon Stone," Bolan said, not bothering to offer his hand. "I'm helping out Homeland Security with an issue." When Kingston didn't say anything, he offered up his credentials.

Kingston shrugged. "What's DHS want now? You need more airport screeners?" He laughed.

Bolan considered his response for a moment, then said, "Some things are better done off the books. Surely a man who served in the Seventh knows that."

Kingston nodded, his face turning serious. "Yeah, all right. What can I do for you, Brandon?"

"That's Colonel, if you don't mind."

Kingston's jaw clenched again and his lips pursed, keeping something unsaid. "All right, *Colonel*. What can I do for you?"

"DHS got a confirmed report from Border Patrol of U.S. Army weapons being moved in the desert, northwest of Douglas. Since this is the only Army base in the area, they figured it might be a good place to start asking some questions." Bolan eyed Kingston for a minute. "Hard questions."

For a moment, Kingston looked like he'd swallowed a bug—a big, crunchy one—then he shook his head. "Damn it. I don't believe it. Are you kidding me or something?"

"Wish I were, Mr. Kingston," Bolan said. "But I'm not."

Kingston slumped into the chair facing the desk. "Shit," he said, shaking his head. Then he looked at Bolan. "I'm sorry for how I greeted you, Colonel. Truth is, we were told this morning of a surprise audit and facilities inspection for tomorrow morning, so I'm running around like an idiot and short-tempered on top of it. I didn't like surprises when I served in the Seventh, and I like them even less now."

Sensing the man's attitude changing, Bolan nodded. "Consider it forgotten," he said. "We all have bad days, and I don't want to make yours worse. Still, I've got a job to do. If those weapons came from this base, we need to know it and we need to know how."

"You're completely right," Kingston said. "I've never

had anything like this happen before. I'll do everything I can to help you—just name it."

"Seems to me the best place to start would be with an inventory," Bolan said. "If nothing is missing, then that will answer at least one question."

Kingston nodded. "All right. Let me get through this inspection tomorrow morning, then in the afternoon I'll go over our warehouses and inventory logs with a fine-toothed comb. If something has gone missing, we'll find it."

"Sounds good," Bolan said. "In the meantime, I'll be out with the Border Patrol. We're going to take another look at the site where the weapons were found and see if we can start piecing together the movements. I'll get in touch with you by tomorrow night or early the next morning to see what you've discovered."

"I'd appreciate that," Kingston said. "If these weapons are coming out of here, I want to know it. Then the bastards behind it can pay the tab."

"I couldn't agree more," Bolan said. "Thanks for your cooperation."

"Anytime, Colonel," he said, getting to his feet. He stuck out a hand. "I know I was a bit of ass when you came in, but I'd like to offer you my hand and my help."

The two men shook and Bolan thanked him once more before leaving the building—through the office doors this time—and headed back to his car. Rivers was waiting for him back in Douglas, and they had a long day ahead of them.

RENE SURENO WATCHED from the balcony as his second, Jesus Salazar, drilled the small group of men in hand-to-hand combat. Rene allowed himself a grim chuckle. For a man named after the son of God, Jesus was anything but a pacifist. He was an icy killing machine who'd served in the Mexican army for several years before traveling to Africa and working for a private military company as a mercenary.

Rene had hired him after Jesus had returned to Mexico and run afoul of one of his distributors. The distributor and several of Rene's men showed up for months in little pieces all over Mexico City. Rene was no fool and knew that any man capable of that would be a powerful ally, and he'd been right. For the right amount of money, Jesus would do almost anything, but for the past several months, he'd been focused on moving drugs and weapons while training Rene's soldiers to kill and fight better than any other cartel in the country.

He watched as Jesus quickly defeated a man by dropping him to the hard stones of the courtyard in one swift move and sweeping his legs out from beneath him. As the man lay there, he simulated the finishing move that in real combat would have killed him—dropping an elbow into his throat, then following with a reverse move with his knife that would have opened his neck from one side to the other. Getting to his feet, Jesus turned his attention to the others, explaining why the man had lost.

As Jesus spoke, the man got slowly to his feet and Rene saw the hate in his eyes—and realized his intentions—before Jesus would have had a chance to notice. Drawing his combat knife, the man lunged forward, then stopped cold as the bullet from Rene's gun took him in the abdomen. The echo from the shot startled everyone, and they looked up at the balcony to see him staring down into the courtyard.

Jesus turned and saw the would-be killer falling to

the ground, then moved closer, kicking the knife out of his hands. *"Gracias,"* he called up to Rene. *"Podría haber sido doloroso."*

"Painful?" Rene laughed. "He might have killed you." He preferred to speak in English, knowing that disappearing inside the U.S. required the ability to speak without an accent.

"Maybe," Jesus admitted. "But I knew you were there." He looked down at the man groaning and bleeding on the stones. "It's never personal," he said, loud enough for the others to hear. "You cannot let it be personal. This man allowed his anger to get the better of his judgment. See what it cost him?"

The other soldiers agreed quite loudly that the man had made a mistake. "You two," Jesus said, gesturing at two men nearby. "Get him out of here. Put him in the hot box." Eyes wide at this cruelty, the men did as they were told, and Jesus turned his attention back to the fighters he'd been training.

Rene contemplated having the man killed outright, but Jesus's choice would send a clear message—those foolish enough to bite the hand that fed them would not just be killed, but would die horribly. Behind him, the phone on his desk rang, and he turned his attention back inside, shutting the balcony doors behind him.

"Hello?" he said, picking up the handset.

"Rene, this is Kingston. We have a problem."

"What problem?" Rene asked, annoyed. Kingston had proven useful to his weapon smuggling plans and was even more helpful with information. Still, he could be overly jumpy, and he was only one cog in the chain. Paranoia had its place, but a man should still be able to sleep at night.

"There's a guy sniffing around where he doesn't belong. He'll be with that Border Patrol agent who interrupted our last shipment."

"They're going back?" Rene asked.

"Yes, so I've heard."

"I'll take care of it. You keep working on the next shipment."

"Don't you want to let things cool off a bit?" Kingston asked. "We can't afford to get caught."

"Shut up," Rene snarled. "I said I will take care of this man. You just do your job. Everything stays on schedule. Understood?"

The silence stretched for several seconds. "Understood," he replied.

"Good," Rene said, then hung up the phone. He returned to the balcony and called Jesus inside. They had some planning to do.

Dinner the night before with Rivers and his young family had reinforced Bolan's opinion of the man—he was one of the good guys. His wife, Olivia, was a down-to-earth, dark-haired, dark-eyed beauty from a wealthy Greek family. They had a wonderful eight-year-old daughter, Katrina, who was the spitting image of her mother and had the laugh of an angel. Bolan was charmed by the little girl. Her dark eyes stared directly into his as she asked very adult questions about everything from where he was born to why he carried such a big gun. The evening had been a pleasure, with good food and laughter and the sharing of peaceful company—a situation Bolan valued more with each passing day of his life. Colton Rivers was obviously a family man of the first order.

Early the next morning, Bolan found himself some black coffee and a woman selling warm tortillas and eggs from a hot cart near his hotel. He drank the coffee and ate his breakfast while he waited for Rivers to arrive. Once he did, they headed out of town, following Highway 80 West, then cutting north toward Tombstone. Rivers explained that there was a lot of big empty nothing out there—mountains, desert, cacti and the occasional cougar hunting free-range cattle when the opportunity arose. "And in between Bisbee, Tombstone and Sierra Vista, there's an area of about a hundred square miles where we've seen a lot of illegal traffic in the past year or so."

"You do flyovers, right?" Bolan asked.

Rivers nodded. "Sure, but it's a big desert and we've got limited resources. The only reason we were out that night is because one of the unmanned drones picked up some unidentified movement during the day that was too big to be humans. We figured maybe a couple of mules—the guys who run illegals up into Tucson or Phoenix—had some trucks out there."

Ten miles or so outside of Tombstone, Rivers cut back west, using a dirt track that made the one Tony lived on look like a well-maintained, big-city street.

"The San Pedro Conservation area is about ten miles west of here, but it gets a lot of tourist traffic—bird watchers, mostly—so the illegals tend to avoid it." Rivers pointed to a series of large, rocky hills in the distance. "That's where we were when they hit us."

Bolan nodded, glad he'd brought his sunglasses along. The desert sun was reflecting off every light-colored surface and would have been blinding without them. "Let's start there, then," he said. "I want to see where you were positioned."

Rivers guided the SUV around rocks, saguaro cacti, a few stunted mesquite trees and plenty of low, pointy scrub brush. The wandering route made Rivers chuckle. "Tony says that everything out here will stick you, prick you or kill you. Some of those damn Mesquite needles will puncture a tire."

They were within a couple hundred yards of the rocky

terrain. "This is close enough," Bolan said. "You came in this way with your men, right?"

"More or less," Rivers replied. "There's hardly a path."

"Let's walk from here," Bolan suggested.

The agent shrugged and pulled the SUV to a stop, cutting off the engine. Both men climbed out and into the staggering heat. Rivers unpacked a shotgun from the back and offered it to him, but he shook his head. It wouldn't make sense for any of the illegals to still be in the area after the recent firefight. Their operations depended on not getting caught in the open.

They moved across the intervening terrain, and Bolan noted that there were plenty of tire tracks and crushed plants to show how much vehicle movement had occurred in the area. "Are all of these from your guys?" he asked, gesturing at the imprints in the sand.

Rivers nodded. "We had to bring in a flatbed to pull our vehicles, plus the ambulance and field people. It was a goddamn mess."

"I bet," Bolan said, scanning the horizon. They were in a lousy position, and although he didn't expect trouble, it never paid to be stupid about such things. They climbed up the rocky hillside and surveyed the lee where the ambush had happened. There was still plenty of evidence that a little gate into hell had opened down there.

"They were moving over there when we spotted them," Rivers said, pointing to the valley floor and another, still larger set of rocks and hills, perhaps three-quarters of a mile or a little farther away. "We checked it out the next day. They left some tracks, but we still haven't figured out how they got there."

"Odd," Bolan said, thinking. The agents' post was

a good place to watch the area, with plenty of cover. "I'm trying to figure out how they got so close to your position."

"It happened damn fast, Matt," Rivers said. "I saw them moving around and they disappeared. We were getting ready to pull out, and I saw them again, and then *bam,* they were on us."

"Maybe—" Bolan started to say when a shot rang out, and the back of Rivers's head exploded in a gruesome shower of blood, bone and brain.

Diving for cover, the Executioner cursed to himself. The Border Patrol agent was dead before his body hit the ground, and now Bolan was out here without any backup and no idea where the shot had come from. He rolled to a well-protected spot behind a cluster of rocks and drew the Desert Eagle from his shoulder rig. Unfortunately, the round that had killed Rivers was from a rifle, and a handgun was not a long-distance weapon.

He heard scuffling feet and rolling rocks and turned, scanning in every direction. From the far side of another collection of boulders, a voice called, "Do you want to die, too, *gringo?*"

The sounds of movement were now surrounding him from all sides, and Bolan knew he was in real trouble. "Not really," he called. His assailants had him cornered. All they were trying to do now was avoid casualties on their end. "On the other hand, I'm happy to take some of you with me if this gets out of hand."

The man Bolan presumed was the speaker stepped out from his cover. He had a Heckler & Koch sniper rifle over his shoulder and was now pointing a simple, tactical shotgun on Bolan. He wasn't a big man, but he was compactly built, with the lean muscle and steady gaze that said he was not a man to screw with.

"You don't have to die today," the man said. "But if you don't throw down your weapon, you will."

Bolan nodded and got slowly to his feet. He had considered fighting back, but the moment Rivers hit the ground, he'd decided that would be counterproductive. He was alone and outnumbered, and allowing himself to be captured would give him access to the people behind all of this.

"Easy," Bolan said. He dropped the magazine out of the Desert Eagle, then worked the slide, emptying the chamber. He reversed the gun and held it out butt-first to the man. "It's my favorite, so I'd just as soon not throw it on the ground."

The man nodded and whistled softly. Six more men appeared from hiding, their weapons trained on Bolan, who kept his hands up. "I understand," the man said, moving in and taking the weapon from him. "I'll see that it's well taken care of."

"I'd appreciate it," Bolan said. "What now?"

"Now?" the man said. "We drive."

BOLAN WAS IN the back of a truck that was rattling along on either a rutted dirt road or barely a road at all. He was blindfolded, and his hands were tied together with plastic zip ties, as were his ankles. The men had searched him, confiscating his wallet, keys and the other documents he had on him.

Gritting his teeth at a massive bump, Bolan tried to hold himself as still as possible and replay the day's events in his mind. He'd been too casual, thinking the ambush Rivers had called him about was most likely someone—maybe a single individual—selling weapons to a small cartel, who had panicked when confronted by the Border Patrol. Maybe both sides had panicked—it had been dark and confusing. Bolan had underestimated the situation and those involved, and it had cost someone, a good man, his life.

Rivers was dead, and Bolan had to accept some of the responsibility for that. Owning your mistakes, he knew, was at least as important as owning your successes, maybe even more so. He intended to do everything he could not only to put an end to whatever was really going on, but also to ensure that Rivers hadn't died in vain. Someone had a bill to pay, and the Executioner intended to collect in full.

It seemed like a smart bet that he'd been taken into Mexico, though he couldn't know for sure how far they'd come. He estimated they'd been driving for at least two hours when the truck slowed, turned and then rolled to a stop.

Bolan heard the tarp covering the back end of the truck get shoved aside, and then his blindfold was ripped off. Several faces peered in at him—every look one of contempt and anticipated violence. Two large men reached in, grabbed him by the ankles and dragged him out into the midday sun. Once he was clear of the tailgate, they hoisted him into the air like a trussed-up turkey and pulled him forward. The toes of his boots trailed dust in his wake.

Bolan did his best to stay upright and scan his surroundings. They'd obviously brought him into the courtyard of an old hacienda. Many of the buildings were little more than basic adobe structures, with no windows and blankets for doors. He saw the main house at the far end of the courtyard, and it was either much newer than the adobe huts or had been massively renovated. Second-floor balconies overlooked the compound below, and on the roof he spotted heavy air-conditioning units and several satellite dishes.

Bolan's two escorts came to a halt before a small structure, not much larger than an outhouse. One of the men opened the door, and the other tossed him inside, then slammed it shut, leaving Bolan in near total darkness.

Bolan readjusted his position, knowing that if he struggled, his bonds would only get tighter. He flexed his wrists and ankles, trying to get the blood flowing into his aching limbs. The hospitality of this particular group of thugs left a great deal to be desired. He closed his eyes, taking in several deep breaths.

That was when he noticed he wasn't alone.

6

It was the copper scent of blood that first alerted Bolan's senses to another presence. In the dim light, it took him several seconds to establish that his cellmate was alive, if barely. His chest rose and fell in stuttering stops and starts. Scooting along the floor, Bolan moved closer, trying to see if there was any hope for the man.

From what he could tell, short of an emergency room and an operating table, the man was too far gone. Blood caked his abdomen in a thick layer. He didn't stir, even when Bolan nudged him gently and asked, "How badly are you hurt?" in both English and Spanish.

Giving up, he leaned back against the wall, doing his best to stretch out his legs. The cell was stifling, and what little fresh air had entered when they'd tossed him in was being rapidly overwhelmed by the heat. He realized that the cell was a hot box, like the kinds used in harsh prisons for solitary confinement. A tiny slot at the top of the door let in the only light, and the structure itself was made from heavy, dried oak rather than adobe. It was like being inside a wood oven, and left there too long, a person would die from heat stroke.

Bolan passed the time reviewing everything Rivers had told him, as well as what little he'd seen before he'd been captured and on his brisk afternoon drag to the hot box. It wasn't much to go on, but it was something. His instincts told him that the man he'd spoken to earlier wasn't the boss, but an underling sent on a specific mission. It was also a safe bet that this wasn't just a simple weapon-smuggling ring, but a much larger operation.

Whether they dealt in weapons, drugs or human trafficking, Mexican cartels were not known for their merciful qualities. They functioned in a world of violence and death, where only the very strong survived. Cartel leaders regularly killed those who crossed them—police and journalists were favorite targets—and those who disobeyed orders often suffered the same fate.

Which was why Bolan had been surprised by the man he'd spoken to in the desert. He didn't carry the weapon of a typical cartel thug, and he didn't act like one, either. That HK looked brand new, and it was the kind of sniper rifle used by advanced military forces. Bolan guessed the man was a paid mercenary with real field experience. He might be even more dangerous than the big boss, though whether the big boss knew it or believed it was another matter entirely.

He'd been sweating for about two hours when the guards came for him, and Bolan put up little resistance as they ordered him to his feet. Beads of sweat stung his eyes, and as he was trying to get his bearings, the zip ties on his ankles were cut loose. Blood flowed back into his feet with a sharp, burning sensation, but he was grateful nonetheless.

"Get moving," the man holding his arm said. "To the main house."

"Are you sure we couldn't stop at a bar for a cold beer?" he asked. "I'm kind of thirsty."

The guard had the good grace to laugh. "No *cerveza* for you, my friend. Mr. Sureno wants to talk to you."

Sureno, Bolan thought. This was progress. They reached the house and climbed a short flight of steps to a large door. When they entered, Bolan felt the cooling breath of air conditioning and sighed in relief. It wasn't something cold to drink, but it was at least a better environment and helped clear his head.

He was guided through the foyer and down the hall, then into a room that looked to be a study. It housed comfortable furniture in the form of two couches and several overpadded chairs, and the walls were lined with bookshelves. Most of the far wall was made up of windows that looked out into a small flower garden. In the middle of it, Bolan could see a fountain with clear water bubbling up through the top.

At one end of the room was a simple desk, and the man seated behind it rose to his feet. "Ah, our guest," he said. "You can cut the ties on his wrists," he told the guard. "I'm perfectly safe."

"Sir?"

"Do it," the man said, his voice sharpening just the slightest bit.

The man sat down again as the guard cut Bolan's hands free. He moved them from behind his back, gently stretching his shoulders and working his wrists to get the blood flowing again. "Thank you," he said, meaning it. Although he had every intention of taking this man down, the time wasn't right. He had no reason to play the antagonist—at least not yet.

The man nodded and waited for the guard to leave the room. Once they were alone, he gestured for Bolan to sit and poured two glasses of water from a pitcher on

the desk, keeping one and passing the other to Bolan.
"Drink," he said, sipping some of the icy water to show
that it wasn't poisoned. "The hot box can suck the life
out of a man in a very short time. You must be thirsty."

"It's not the coldest place I've ever been," Bolan said,
picking up the glass and drinking deeply. He imagined
that if he'd been in the cell much longer, he might be
gulping straight from the pitcher. When he finished, he
set the glass back down and looked at the man on the
other side of the desk. He wore a nice suit—not tailored,
but well cut. "Mr. Sureno, I presume?" Bolan said.

"Yes. Rene Sureno." He opened a drawer and pulled
out Bolan's wallet. "And according to this, you're Matt
Cooper."

Bolan nodded, wondering what they'd done with his
Colonel Stone credentials. Surely someone had noticed
he'd been carrying two sets of identification. "That's
me."

"Yet you are not with the Border Patrol and you don't
carry identification from any other law enforcement
agency I know of. How is it that you were in the desert
working with them?"

He shrugged. "I do some consulting work from time
to time."

"Consulting?" Sureno asked, laughing. "And what is
it you consult on?"

"Investigative consulting," Bolan replied. "Mostly
how something could have been done when no one else
has a clue how."

"I'm afraid I don't believe you, Mr. Cooper," Sureno
said. "But I suppose we must start somewhere. What
were you doing out in the desert with that border patrol agent?"

"Asking questions," Bolan said. "That's what investigators do. Those weapons they found in the desert in that little action the other day were military."

Sureno nodded. "Yes, a sad loss. And expensive in terms of the equipment and the men killed that night."

"Seemed like a lot of loss on both sides, if you ask me."

"Perhaps, but there will always be more Border Patrol agents, and I can get more men. But there is a limited supply of weapons at any one time." He tsked sadly to himself. "Well, it's the cost of doing business in this dangerous time."

"It's never easy running a business," Bolan said. "Of course, in your line of work, I imagine there are more dangers than those faced by, say, a grocery store or a gas station."

Sureno chuckled again. "You are a man of wit, I see. Humor is a salve to the soul, but it's not very effective in the hot box, Mr. Cooper. So, I'm going to ask you my questions again, and this time, I urge you to answer them honestly. If you don't..." He shrugged. "Then I will have Jesus ask you, and he is not as kind as I am. He is not kind at all."

"Jesus?" Bolan asked, knowing this was about to turn ugly. "As in the son of God? He works for you, too?"

Sureno laughed once more. "Not quite," he admitted. "Now, tell me again why a man with no agency identification is working with the Border Patrol."

Before Bolan could answer, the door to the study opened. "He won't tell you," the man from the desert said. "I wouldn't, and neither will...Colonel Stone, is it?"

"I prefer Matt Cooper, but if you like Colonel Stone, I can live with that, too."

"Is that the name of the man Kingston ran into at the base, Jesus?" Sureno asked.

The mercenary stepped across the room to stand next to the desk. "It is," he said. "And unless I am very wrong, he's probably Army Criminal Investigations Division, working undercover. Using his actual military identification to get onto the base was a mistake, however."

Bolan's mind raced. If they believed him to be with Army CID, it might change their reactions, and not in a good way.

"What do you have to say to that, Colonel?" Sureno asked. "Is what Jesus says true?"

Knowing what was coming next, Bolan did the only thing he could. "I believe in Jesus, but this man's full of shit."

Sureno smiled, shaking his head. "Let's move him to the interrogation room, Jesus," he said. "We need to learn the truth of this man."

Bolan stood, but Jesus moved in, sweeping his feet from beneath him. Knowing resistance could cost him dearly in this situation, Bolan allowed himself to be trussed with zip ties once more.

Sureno waited patiently while the guards came back, picked Bolan up and carried him out of the room and down the hall to a door that opened into a room that was little more than four concrete walls, a tile floor and a few folding chairs surrounding a stainless steel table.

"Ah, the interrogation room," Bolan said. "I was expecting more of a dungeon decor."

Jesus slapped him. "You talk when I tell you to talk."

The guards shoved Bolan into one of the chairs, and Jesus sat down across from him. As Sureno entered the room and removed his suit coat, Bolan reminded himself that this man wasn't like any Mexican cartel or weapons smuggler he'd ever dealt with. Still, he was willing to bet that as long as Sureno believed he was withholding useful information, he'd be kept alive.

Knowing he was alone out here, that Brognola wouldn't be sending in the cavalry any minute now, would have depressed most men. For the Executioner, it was fuel to the fire. Whatever Sureno was up to with those weapons, Bolan intended to live long enough to burn the operation—and the man—to the ground.

"Are you ready to answer my questions, Colonel Stone?" Sureno asked, leaning down to look in his eyes.

"Not so much," Bolan said.

Sureno laughed again and even Jesus joined in. "He will be hard to break," the mercenary said.

"I suspect you are right," Sureno replied, calmly removing his tie. "It will be interesting to find out what it will take, my friend, but we *will* find out. Every man can be broken."

7

Sureno and Jesus were men of their word. So far, they'd certainly tried to break him, but the Executioner had suffered worse. Physical torture, in Bolan's experience, was one of the least effective ways to get information.

He'd been under interrogation for about an hour when the door flew open and a whirlwind feminine form entered the room.

"I can't believe you brought him here! What were you thinking?" the woman asked.

The guards snickered, and the astonishment on Sureno's face was quickly replaced with a sneer. He swung his arm, the back of his hand connecting with her cheek and knocking her to the ground. Her cry was met with a grunt of approval, and Sureno crouched on the ground next to her.

"You have something to say, *chica?*"

"I was…"

He grabbed her by the throat, lifted her to her feet, then shoved her into the wall. He backhanded her again. Her lip split this time, and a thin spray of blood hit the white wall.

"Something to say?" Sureno hissed.

"No, *mi amor,*" she said, shaking her head.

Bolan wanted nothing more than to break every bone in Sureno's hand, but at the moment, he could only watch, hoping the beating would end. He despised a man who would harm a woman for no reason other than to exert his power over her, to demean her.

Sureno released his hold on her and she slumped to the floor. *"Vámonos!"* he ordered, and the guards stalked out of the room with their boss and Jesus bringing up the rear. The woman remained on the floor. The room was silent and dark lit only by the single bulb hanging from a beam overhead.

"Are you okay?" Bolan asked.

He could hear her weeping quietly and then she got slowly to her feet and shuffled across the floor toward him. The marks for her interference on his behalf were rapidly becoming evident as the swelling increased. She'd have a couple of bruises for her trouble. Behind them, however, was a pretty face, with large, dark eyes, high cheekbones and an olive complexion that would make most women envious.

"I will live," she said. "Rene is…"

"Don't try and sell me the nice guy story," he said. "I'm not buying."

She offered a bitter laugh. "He's not a nice man," she agreed.

Bolan cleared his throat. Now that he knew who and where Sureno was, it was past time to leave and bring in some serious firepower to take him out. "Look, I've got to get out of here," he said. "You could come with me. I have friends who can help us."

"Do you have an army of them?" she asked.

"As a matter of fact, I do," he replied evenly. "With

better weapons and training than anything your so-called boyfriend might put in the field."

She shook her head, obviously not believing him. "He is not my boyfriend. Rene has friends in high places and many men, all trained by Jesus. I knew he was doing bad things on the border, but he's never brought the trouble here."

"What's your name?"

"Isabel."

"Isabel, this is all going to end very badly for Rene, whether he kills me or not. I don't think you want to be in the crossfire when that happens. Let's get both of us out of here."

"I…I cannot leave," she said, looking over her shoulder as though Sureno might be standing behind her.

"That's not true," he said. "Even if you don't help me, you should help yourself and escape."

Isabel hesitated, then put a hand into a pocket in her skirt and pulled out a pearl-handled straight razor. She quickly sliced through his bonds, and he lowered his arms.

"Thank you," he said. "I've got to go. Come with me."

"I don't think you'll make it past Rene's guards, but you're welcome to try. I have…family here that needs to be protected."

"Look, we can come back for them—better armed and better prepared," he argued.

She shook her head. "No, but think kindly of me when—if—you return."

Giving up, he said, "Fine. How do I get out of here?"

"The truck they brought you in on is still parked by the gate. They leave the keys in it. If you can get to it, the gate is kept open during the day… Take this, if it will help," she added, handing Bolan the razor.

"Thank you," he said, slipping it into his boot.

"No matter what happens, you *cannot* let them know I'm involved," Isabel said. "They must not suspect me." Her eyes were pleading, even though her words sounded calm. Now her womanly beauty was replaced by the look of a frightened child.

"This is about more than your family," Bolan said, making a guess. "Who are you and why are you really helping me?"

She looked over her shoulder once more, then leaned in close enough to whisper in his ear. *"Policía Federal Ministerial,"* she said.

Damn it, Bolan thought. She's an undercover cop for the Mexican feds. "You can't leave," he said. "I understand."

"Gracias," she said.

"Get down on the floor," he ordered. "Tell them I got loose and knocked you out. They'll be too busy looking for me to think about you for very long."

She nodded, slumping to the floor near the table. "Thank you," he said again, lowering his voice as footsteps and voices sounded in the hall outside.

"Buena suerte," she whispered. *"Vaya con dios."*

He slid silently behind the door, waiting for the guards to enter. Two men stepped into the room, and the Executioner jumped into action. The straight razor slit the throat of the first man, spraying blood in a huge arc across the room. His shout of surprise was cut short as the blade severed his vocal cords.

The other guard, now covered in blood, spun and tried to draw his gun, but Bolan was faster. Dropping the first man to the floor, he stepped close, driving an elbow into his solar plexus. As the man leaned forward, gasping for breath, Bolan twisted, bringing the razor around again. It entered the guard's body just below the navel, and he sliced upward, opening his abdomen up to the sternum. Most of the man's intestines spilled out onto the floor with a wet splat before he'd even realized what happened.

The guard tried to scream, but without a connected diaphragm, he was unable to do more than drop to his knees, panting in shock as he died. Bolan took his side-arm, a well-cared-for little 9 mm from some off-brand company, then stepped through the door, shutting it behind him. The entire fight had lasted perhaps ten seconds, but now armed—and angry—the Executioner was ready for more.

He had underestimated Sureno but wouldn't do so again. Now was the time to escape, but he would be coming back to avenge Rivers's death as much as for any indignity he'd suffered at the Mexican's hands. And to make sure that Jesus was out of business, too. There was a place in the world for mercenaries, men and women who used their skills to fight the good fight, but serving drug cartels and weapons smugglers…bringing harm to the innocent…that wasn't it.

The hallway was dark and sunset was rapidly approaching. He needed to retrieve his handheld, his wallet and, ideally, his weapon, and the last place he'd seen them was on Sureno's desk. Bolan knew that the element of surprise would only help for a brief window of time. He'd also need a little luck. He moved down the hall quickly, pausing to listen at the office door.

Hearing nothing, he eased the door open. The study

was empty, and he stepped inside. Crossing to the desk, he found his belongings. He slipped the handheld into one pocket and his wallet and identification into another, then grabbed the Desert Eagle, using his shoulder rig for the 9 mm. Sureno didn't keep a computer here, and Bolan saw little else that might be of help. He moved back to the door just as the knob started to turn.

Typical, he thought, sliding behind it and preparing to fight his way out. Sureno entered the office with Jesus on his heels. "We'll go back and finish with Cooper in just a minute," Sureno was saying. "I want to talk with Isabel first. Go and find her."

Jesus turned just as Bolan stepped out from behind the door. "She's unavailable at the moment," he said, aiming the weapon at the mercenary. "You'll just have to wait."

Jesus started to move. "Don't even think it," Bolan snapped. "Whether I kill you now or later makes no difference to me. Neither one of you moves, and you might live through this."

Sureno had turned at the sound of his voice. "How did you…"

"Escape?" Bolan finished. "I'm tricky that way, but I'm afraid I left a bit of a mess in your interrogation room." He shook his head in mock sadness. "All that blood. And poor Isabel—maybe you shouldn't have left her behind. Wrong place, wrong time, I guess."

"If you've harmed her…"

"Shut it, Sureno," Bolan snapped. Jesus was still silent, but he once again moved to Bolan's right. "Don't do it, my friend." He stopped once more, eyeing Bolan with cold regard.

Bolan gestured with the gun at Jesus. "Take the zip ties out of your pocket. You know what to do."

Jesus pulled a handful of zip ties from the cargo pocket of his pants and shrugged. He used one on Sureno's wrists. "Take a seat," Bolan said, pointing to the nearest couch. Sureno sat and Jesus did the same, using another zip tie on his own hands and pulling it tight with his teeth.

"You should kill me, Cooper," Jesus said, eyeing him again. "If you don't, I'm going to kill you when I find you. And you'll die badly, like a wounded animal in the desert."

"Yeah, I'm sure," Bolan said. "You're a badass." He inspected their wrists, then used the remaining zip ties to cuff their ankles together. Satisfied, he took a step back, considering how long it would take to get out of the house and into the courtyard to the truck. The clock was running and he knew that more guards could show up at any second.

"Do yourself a favor, Sureno. Get rid of your attack dog here and go into another line of work. When I come back, if you're still in operation, I'm going to burn you to the ground."

Sureno smiled. "You are assuming you will escape. It's a long way from here to the border, but if you do come back, Mr. Cooper, we will be most happy to host you again."

"I'm counting on it," Bolan replied. Although he could kill both men now, it would bring every man in the compound on the run. He'd never make it out alive, and someone else would rise from the ashes to take over. When this was finished, he wanted the entire operation gone, never to return. Now wasn't the time, but it would come.

Bolan opened the door enough to glance into the hallway, then turned back to Sureno. "Start yelling or raise a fuss, and I'll be forced to come back in here. I may die, but you will, too. I'll make sure of it." He stepped out of the room, shut the door, then broke off the handle on his side.

He walked quickly toward the main door, keeping the Desert Eagle tucked next to his leg. He was halfway down the front steps before the alarms went off— old-school sirens like those used to warn a neighborhood of an incoming tornado or air raid. Men began running in all directions, obviously drilled for what to do.

Bolan moved more rapidly himself, following a group of men headed for the gate. He saw the truck and angled in that direction, just reaching the tailgate when he heard shouting from the house. "There! You damn fools! He's right there!"

Risking a quick glance over his shoulder, he saw that Jesus was standing in the doorway and lifting an assault rifle to open fire. Bolan dove forward, rolling and twisting, just as the spray of bullets tore into the ground and metal tailgate of the truck.

8

Bolan crawled along the side of the truck to the driver's side door. Bullets whined around him, penetrating metal and dirt. He could only pray that one of them didn't hit the radiator or the engine block. He reached the door and pulled himself into the cab, keeping low as more men closed in on the vehicle.

"Time to go," he said, turning the key.

He didn't wait for the men to figure it out, just shoved the transmission into drive and floored it, sitting up only enough to steer. The next wave of bullets shattered every window in the cab, covering him in safety glass. Two guards were shoving the gate closed, but Bolan didn't even slow down. One managed to jump out of the way, but the other wasn't quite fast enough. The front end of the truck clipped him, no doubt breaking his leg by the sound of his agonized screams.

As Bolan cleared the wall of the compound, he sat up and guided the truck down the road. There was only one way to go at the moment, and unfortunately, the road wasn't going north but east. Still, he was out and alive, and now it was just a matter of getting away.

He glanced in the rearview mirror and could see the dust rising from the compound as vehicles moved in pursuit. He knew he was just as visible as they were, and with a lead of less than a mile, he wasn't in the clear yet. Not even close.

"Damn," he muttered, scanning the horizon for something like cover. He looked in the rearview once more and saw a chopper lifting over the walls of the compound. "A bonus," he said, glad for his weapons. A couple of handguns and a straight razor wouldn't hold out long against assault rifles, but a man made do with what he had. Seeing nothing in the distance, the Executioner made a decision.

He yanked the wheel hard left, leaving the rutted road and cutting north. The closer he got to the border—and he had no idea how far away it might be—the better chance he had of being spotted by someone in a position to help or at least come investigate. The truck rattled fiercely as he maneuvered around rocks and mesquite trees. This way was slower, but it would be slower for his pursuers too.

All of them, he thought, except the chopper. He could hear it now, closing the gap rapidly. If he were a betting man, he'd wager that Jesus was on it, most likely carrying some seriously badass hardware. Off to his right, Bolan spotted a wash where a riverbed had long since gone dry, and he turned into it. The walls would help hide his dust trail from the vehicles giving chase, and it would make it harder for the chopper to get close.

The walls of the wash rose up on either side of him, and he was now heading in a northeasterly direction. Not perfect, but the ground was relatively flat and obstacle free, allowing him to push his speed higher. He was contemplating his next move when the first hail of bullets from whoever was riding shotgun in the chopper kicked up dirt and pinged off the body of the truck.

Bolan swerved, trying to make himself a more difficult target, but without cover, it wasn't going to do much good. More rounds pinged off the roof of the truck, and several passed through, hitting the dashboard. The chopper was right on top of him. It was only a matter of time until he took a bullet—or the truck did—and then the chase would be over.

Making a quick decision, Bolan slammed on the brakes. The pilot didn't have time to correct. He flew past Bolan's position as he gunned the truck again. The Executioner drew his Desert Eagle and fired through the shattered windshield, aiming for the man he could see hanging halfway out the open door of the passenger compartment. Disappointed that it wasn't Jesus, he still knew that one less enemy at this point—especially one shooting at him—was a good thing.

The passenger was busy shouting at the pilot. Bolan's first two rounds were a bit off, but the sudden attack caused the pilot to veer up, giving him a clear shot. The Executioner fired a third time, and his round took the man high in the chest. He briefly grappled for something to hold onto, then fell from the chopper, landing in a heap in front of the stolen truck.

Bolan braked again and jumped out, ready to put another round into the man should he still be alive, but it was unnecessary. Whether it was the shot or the fall that did the job, he was dead. But his assault rifle, a Colt M4 carbine, seemed intact. Most likely, this one had also been stolen from the U.S. Army. With the chopper turning back toward him, Bolan put his Desert Eagle away and picked up the Colt, checking the magazine and doing a fast visual inspection.

The weapon was undamaged. Bolan grabbed two more magazines from the dead man, then returned to the truck. Another man was visible in the front of the chopper, sitting next to the pilot, and a second shooter was now hanging out the open door. Bolan didn't hesitate. He pulled the Colt to his shoulder and opened up. He put his first few rounds into the chopper's windscreen. The pilot pulled up immediately, veering away from Bolan's position in the wash.

The maneuver put the shooter in view, and Bolan fired twice, hitting him clean both times. He fell backward into the cabin. Still firing, the Executioner put several more rounds into the aircraft and saw smoke start to billow from the back rotors and the telltale flicker of gasoline leaking out of the fuel tank. The chopper lurched back and forth as the pilot struggled for control, and Bolan watched as it went down a mile or so away.

He considered his options, then reached a decision. Given the number of men headed his way—it looked like four vehicles by the dust plumes he spotted over the edge of the wash, it was time to go on foot. Shouldering the carbine, Bolan looked into the cab for anything that might be useful, especially water, and came up empty. Turning to leave, he realized that he'd overestimated how much time he had. Two more vehicles were closing on him from the opposite direction.

Sureno must have called in some of the men in the field. They were communicating by radio, triangulating his position. Now they were surrounding him. He could try and head due north, but without water or provisions, and no real idea of how far it was to the border, he could die, even if he did elude capture. No, it would be better to do the unexpected.

He began running at a quick clip toward the oncoming vehicles, and when they got to within a hundred yards or so, he pulled the carbine free again and opened up. Both vehicles slammed to a halt and four men, two from each, dived out, taking cover behind the rocks lining the sides of the wash. They were staying down, knowing that all they had to do was wait and he'd be trapped.

Bolan also dove behind a boulder, then glanced back down the wash toward the truck. He'd parked it sideways, so it would give him some cover. At the very least, the men coming from that direction would have to stop and get out of their vehicles. On foot, they'd be slower and more cautious.

He peered around the wash again, hoping to spot something he could use to his advantage. Suddenly, he realized his knees were wet. He looked down and saw that the dirt beneath him was plenty damp. Scanning the wall, he noted that water had cut a path into the side of the wash itself. It wasn't quite a cave, but it just might do.

He dropped lower and slid inside the hollowed-out space, ignoring the stagnant, alkali-scented puddles. He turned, then used the stock of the carbine on the ceiling, angling the barrel into the space he'd crawled through. It only took several quick jabs to bring down dirt in sheets, covering the entrance. Bolan turned the rifle back and forth, then gently removed it from the wet dirt. A hole smaller than a quarter remained, letting in a tiny bit of light, oxygen and, most important, sound.

Now it was just a matter of waiting and striking when the moment was right.

MORE THAN AN hour passed. Bolan couldn't see out of the hole, but he could hear. Sureno's men walked past several times. They were stumped as to where he'd gone, and despite sending out men to look, they'd come up empty—which was understandable, considering that he hadn't gone anywhere.

As they were debating what to do and arguing about whose fault it was, he heard the faint crackle of a radio, then the familiar voice of Jesus asking for an update. Taking a risk, Bolan pressed himself closer to the small hole, trying to see. From what he could tell, they'd gathered around the man holding the transmitter.

Bolan wasn't going to get a better opportunity. The men had their backs to his position and were less than twenty feet away, gathered in the middle of the wash. He pushed the dirt away from the small opening and switched the selector on the carbine to automatic. Then he cut loose. Men died screaming as bullets filled the air.

Bolan pushed the rest of the soil out of the way, crawling toward his boulder once more. Of the twelve men he spotted, six were down before he'd finished getting out of the little cave. Two more dropped as he made it to the boulder and the magazine on his assault rifle went empty. Rather than reload, he simply dropped it and switched to the Desert Eagle.

Its booming roar filled the air as he took down two men who tried to rush his position. That left two, both of whom had taken cover on the far side of his truck and were shooting wildly, unable to know for sure where he was. Panic was a wonderful field tool. Bolan dashed for the truck, rolling as he got near.

He glimpsed two sets of feet on the far side and pulled the trigger, hitting each man in the lower leg. The powerful weapon all but tore limbs off at this range, and they were screaming in agony as he got to his feet. He worked his way around to the far side and finished the job, cutting off their cries in mid-note. It was more mercy than they'd have shown him.

Bolan scanned the area and saw nothing but bodies. Not all of Sureno's men here were dead, but none of them were long for this world. On the ground near one of them, he spotted the radio and could hear Jesus demanding information. *"Lo que está sucediendo? Que es disparar?"*

He picked it up and keyed the mike. "I was doing the shooting, Jesus," he said. "And that's just the beginning. I'll be seeing you and Sureno real soon." He threw the radio to the ground and moved toward the group of vehicles on the far side of the wash. Bolan wanted to search them quickly before he left, on the chance that he might find some supplies that would help him stay alive on his trek across the desert.

He didn't see the man who'd taken shelter in the backseat of the first car he approached until he lunged forward, gun in hand.

9

The shot creased Bolan's left temple. He fell sideways, hitting the dirt with a thud, and the panicked Mexican continued his lunge out of the car. Bolan fired. The rounds from his Desert Eagle hit the man square in the chest, and he stumbled backward, hitting the door of the car. His surprised stare was sightless as he slumped to the ground.

Bolan climbed slowly to his feet. His head pounded, but the bleeding wasn't too bad for a scalp wound. He tore a strip off his T-shirt and wrapped it around his head, blinking to clear the sweat and blood from his eyes. For now, he'd have to settle for getting away alive. He looked through the two cars and found a half-filled bottle of water on the floor and little else. Bolan surveyed the area once more. He didn't see any plumes of dust indicating that he had more company coming. Still, although taking a vehicle was tempting, it would be easily spotted moving through the desert at a distance. He'd have to remain afoot if he wanted to avoid notice.

To the north, a low line of scrub-covered hills beckoned. If he moved quickly, he might be able to put himself on the far side of them before another, more organized search could be mounted. A look at the sky told him it would be full dark in less than thirty minutes.

Bolan checked that his gear was secured, then headed out, moving as fast as he could toward the hills.

THE JOURNEY BECAME a blur. By midnight, Bolan was suffering from the effects of his day and a lack of water. He'd been dehydrated to begin with, and the chase, gunplay and hike hadn't helped. Several times, Bolan missed a step and fell, once rolling into another washout and crashing through the remains of a dead mesquite tree. The needles stabbed him and tore through his clothes, shredding his skin.

Somehow, he got to his feet, found his bearings again and kept moving. When he stumbled once more and fell to his knees, he felt his consciousness begin to let go. He was about to give in to the darkness when he heard footsteps behind him. Mustering his strength, Bolan spun around, reaching into his shoulder rig for the Desert Eagle. In the moonlight, he made out the weathered face of an old man.

"Tony."

"Seems like you're having a rough time, my friend," Tony said. "Come with me, and I'll get you sorted."

A wave of relief washed over Bolan. For the moment, he would live.

THE SOUND OF coyotes yipping in the distance, the warm crackle of a fire and the smell of cowboy coffee were the first things to filter into Bolan's consciousness when he awoke. He tried to roll over, but at the first movement his body screamed in protest.

"Welcome back to the land of the living, son."

Bolan jerked semi-upright and regretted it almost immediately. He groaned, and Tony laughed softly.

"I save you from the vultures and you still suspect. That's all right, I'd do the same," the old man said. He sat across from Bolan, sipping from an old enamel mug. He looked peaceful and totally at home. "Guess you're probably thirsty." He stood and knelt next to Bolan, handing him a canteen.

"How did you find me?" Bolan asked.

"Olivia."

Bolan lowered his head. He hadn't had much time to consider Colton Rivers's wife in all of this, but knowing she'd sent Tony meant she knew about her husband and his tragic end. To the east, the sky was turning gray, the first rays of light from a new day. But for her, there would be no sunshine for a long time to come.

"When you two didn't come back, she called the Border Patrol station and they sent out a team. They found the SUV and Colton, but since you aren't here in any official capacity, she didn't have anyone else to turn to. She called me and I set out after you. You want to tell me what happened?"

"I made a mistake," Bolan admitted. "And it got Colton killed. They were waiting for us when I expected them to be long gone. After Colton went down, I didn't have much choice. It was surrender or die, so I let them take me. I figured I could at least do some recon." He shook his head. "Even then, I still thought it was probably just a better-than-usual group of cartel thugs. It wasn't until I met the leader and his right-hand man that I realized how serious the situation was."

"Let me guess," Tony said. "You ran into Rene Sureno." When Bolan nodded, he continued. "I did some digging around, and that was the name I came up with. He's a big player now and on the Mexican government's radar. The problem is that their radar is pretty crowded these days. Anyway, that's how I knew where to start looking for you. His compound is about thirty miles from here."

"Thirty miles?" Bolan repeated, starting to rise. "We need to get moving. They'll find us if we're this close when daylight hits."

"Rest easy, my friend. Rene and his men aren't trackers. I know this country well enough that I could find us a place just outside his gates where we could have a drink, enjoy a campfire and lob grenades over his walls without him knowing where we were." Tony poured himself another cup of coffee. "We'll move on when we've got enough light to see by. Do you know the story of Geronimo?"

"Not the specifics," Bolan said. "Just that he was from around here."

The old man nodded. "This country was Geronimo's, all right. He and his band would raid all along the border, slipping into the valleys on the U.S. side and then use the Chiricahua mountain range to vanish."

Bolan leaned against the rocks and listened to the soft, even rhythm of Tony's voice. Taking small sips from the canteen and popping pieces of dried fruit in his mouth, he allowed himself to relax slightly.

"Finally, the government sent in the cavalry—and I do mean the real thing. The 4th Cavalry was sent out from Fort Huachuca. And Geronimo gave them a merry chase. Whenever it got close, he and his band would hop across the border into Mexico."

"He surrendered eventually, right?"

Tony nodded. "He did, but it was more out of a desire to save what was left of his band. They were beaten by starvation as much as anything else. That and the fact that the 4th never relented once they got going. Either way, many of the trails and camps I use are the very same ones that wily old Apache used." He gestured around them. "This little canyon we're in right now isn't all that far from Rene, especially as the crow flies. But to get in here, you have to be on foot or horseback."

Bolan hadn't realized they had horses with them until that moment. He looked at the two animals, which had been silent the whole time. They were in a makeshift corral nearby.

Tony lifted a small medical bag from the ground and moved closer. "The sun will be up soon. Let's tend to the rest of your wounds." He started at the top, cleaning and using liquid bandages. "I imagine most of these scars I see have a story."

"They do," Bolan said. "But don't they all?"

"Yeah, I figured." He swabbed a particularly nasty cut on Bolan's ribs. "Are you about ready to tell me who you really are?"

"Just as soon as you're ready to do the same," he replied.

"My identity isn't secret," the old man said.

"No, but when Colton told me about you, there were a lot of maybes in the story."

Tony leaned back, examining his work, then nodded with satisfaction. He put the medical bag away, gathering the bits of trash into a plastic bag. Then he dug into a saddlebag and tossed Bolan a clean T-shirt. "Men like you and me, we're like wolves. We know our own kind when we smell 'em."

Bolan chuckled. "I suppose we do. Sureno is a wolf, too, just a different type." His thoughts turned to Rivers once more. "I should've smelled him, but I didn't."

"We all make mistakes," Tony said. "But Sureno isn't a wolf. He's really just a jumped-up coyote. You keep your name, Cooper, but whichever name you use, you'll have a friend here, if you need one. This old man is still good for something every now and then."

Bolan nodded. "You have my thanks. You pulled my fat out of the fire, probably saved my life. I won't forget it."

Tony looked at him carefully. "No," he said, "I don't suppose you will. You aren't that kind of man—or wolf."

"Sureno isn't the forgetting kind, either," Bolan said. "He'll be coming."

10

While waiting for daylight, Bolan and Tony cleaned up the camp, put out the fire and began loading the horses. They were almost finished when the *whip-thip* of helicopter blades cut through the morning air.

"You call in reinforcements?" Bolan asked, suspecting the answer before he heard it.

"Nope. No satellite phone these days." Tony scanned the sky to the south.

"Sureno?"

"Probably," the old man said. "Last I heard, he was strictly a ground crew. When you mentioned that he had a chopper you put down, I figured he's obviously got more toys than I knew about. Let's saddle up. We can lose them in the mountains."

They grabbed the last of the gear on the ground and moved to the horses. Bolan stood out of the way, handing Tony what he needed as he prepped the mounts. Horses were not in his area of expertise. Bolan tied the last of the gear to his horse, then slipped a foot into the stirrup.

"It's been a while since I've done this," he admitted.

"You just hang on to Jesse. She'll stay right with me and Nifty. These girls know the mountains here as well as old Geronimo did. We'll get out of this okay."

Bolan pulled himself into the saddle and turned to follow Tony, who was already marching Nifty up a steep climb. The horses moved carefully as the shale rock gave way under their hooves. They broke through the small stand of trees that was their cover and picked up the pace, trying to get to the next group of trees before they were spotted. The helicopter came soaring over the ridgeline.

"Move!" Bolan shouted.

The sniper from the helicopter rained bullets in their general direction. The horses dug their hooves into the rock and continued up the climb. Bolan clung to the saddle and ducked low, trying to stay clear of the shots.

The helicopter swung around and turned for another pass just as they made the small grove of trees and paused to let the horses breathe. There was far more open country out here than there were good places to hide, and their options were dwindling.

"We're not moving fast enough," Bolan said. "I think we need a distraction."

"What do you have in mind?"

"Do you have any explosives?"

"No, but I know where we can get some. If you can slow the chopper down, I think I can plan a little surprise."

"I can get their attention for a bit," the Executioner said. "Just wait for the shooting to start."

Tony nodded, and Bolan turned in the opposite direction, climbing down from Jesse and tying her loosely to a branch. He moved into the open, and the men spotted him. The chopper swept in low to give the sniper a clear shot. Bolan worked quickly along the tree line, keeping the helicopter in sight, then slipped behind a wide trunk for cover. The sniper took a couple of shots, but luckily the angle was bad.

Taking advantage, Bolan stepped back out and opened up with the carbine. He put several rounds into the main cabin of the craft, and it veered up and away. That should have bought Tony some time, he thought, and he cut back through the trees and gathered his mount. The helicopter hadn't left, but it had pulled out to quite a distance, circling and waiting for him to be visible once more.

Bolan walked Jesse to the far side of the grove, then saddled up and headed after the old man. He crossed the top of the first ridge and looked to the valley below. He could see the dirt clouds from vehicles following along the other side of the hill, searching for an opening to break through.

Bolan kicked Jesse into a full gallop, holding the saddle horn with one hand and the reins with the other, doing his best to stay on and stay low. He'd once heard an old horseman say that when someone was in that position on horse, he was praying, not riding. For the moment, this would have to do. Bolan spotted the glint of Tony's scope and angled Jesse in that direction. The sound of the chopper closing in echoed along the steep red rocks of the canyon.

"Ride hard!" Tony yelled.

Bolan urged Jesse even faster, and then he saw Tony stand up from behind a boulder and raise his rifle in his direction. He ducked as the round whizzed past his head and into the rocks behind him. The explosion blasted the hillside, tossing sharp shards of rock into the air.

The debris rained over Bolan and his mount, and as he heard the sound of the explosion and felt the sting of the rocks hitting him, the horse found even more speed and was running as though all the demons of hell were on her heels. Bolan clung to the saddle with all his strength, and as they reached Tony, he pulled the horse up short, nearly coming out of the saddle as she rocked back on her haunches.

Jesse spun in tight circles, and Bolan saw that the chopper had broken off its pursuit for the moment and was flying back to the south. "What the *hell* was that?" he asked, looking down at the grinning old man.

Tony chuckled and put his rifle back in the saddle scabbard. "Dynamite," he said. "Very old dynamite. All these mountain ranges and hills are covered in old silver mines that either played out or didn't play at all. Once in a while, you can find an old crate of dynamite that was left behind. I make it a point to know where they are."

"How many sticks did you put up there? I thought that whole mountain was going to come down on top of us."

"One," Tony said, climbing into the saddle. "I figured that would be enough."

"Just one, huh?" Bolan asked. "I guess it was plenty. Did you take some for the road?"

Tony shook his head. "No, it's too unstable. Those old sticks sweat nitroglycerin like a horse that's been ridden by a renegade Apache on the run. One bad bump and they'd be finding pieces of us for the next month."

Bolan nodded. "True enough. Still, I'd be happy to have some more options when it comes to weapons. Rifles and handguns aren't much against a chopper with a sniper on board."

"Agreed, but we'll just have to make do. I did plant a small surprise on the top ridge last night, right where those vehicles might try and come across. We'll see if it works."

"What do you mean?"

"I mean it could go off early and do nothing more than block the road for a bit, or it could go off when they spring the trap."

"Why would it go off early?"

Tony nodded at the sky. "The heat alone might be enough to make them blow. Like I said, those old sticks are damn unstable. That's the problem with the stuff— you're taking your life in your hands just touching it. Any number of people have been blown to kingdom come thinking they've found a really cool firework while they're out hiking in the mountains. They'll stick it in a backpack, and before they get all the way down the mountain, the dynamite has begun to sweat. The next little jump or bump, and there's not enough for dental records."

"How much farther until we hit the U.S. border?" Bolan scanned the sky once more, but the chopper was no longer in sight. Maybe some of the debris from the blast had damaged the craft.

"At the rate we're going, we'll make it sometime after nightfall," Tony said.

"Then we'd better get moving," he replied. "The sooner we're back on U.S. soil, the sooner I can take some action against Sureno that's fairly permanent."

Tony chuckled and put his heels to his horse, and Bolan followed closely behind.

The old man knew every hidden pass, rocky crevice and back way out of a box canyon—just as Rivers had said. As they rode, they occasionally heard the sound of the chopper, but it never came close to their position. It amazed Bolan that Sureno hadn't given up the hunt. He was persistent; that much was certain.

The sun had just dropped below the horizon when Tony reined in at the top of a long path leading down and out of the small mountain range. Below, Bolan could see the faint outlines of a valley floor.

"We're almost home," Tony said. "There's a little creek about halfway across that valley that's used to mark the border. Cross that, and we're back on U.S. soil and, at the least, a bit closer to safety."

"That's good," Bolan said, cocking his head to listen, then nodding when the sound echoed more clearly off the rocks around them. "Because here they come again."

"Maybe we'll get lucky," Tony said, spurring his horse forward.

The helicopter came into view, overflying the ridge-line then running close to the ground. Both men tucked low over their saddles and galloped full speed down the mountain and across the valley, which had once been a lake bed. Now, it was little more than patches of scrub and alkali flats. Dust rose around them in choking clouds and the faint taste of salt filled Bolan's mouth.

The helicopter was gaining on them, but they were closing rapidly on the creek. A blue flare lit the sky ahead and Bolan began to veer away from the light, but Tony rode straight for it. "I hope you know what you're doing!" Bolan shouted, staying the course.

"Me, too!" the old man yelled in return.

Behind them, the chopper's bright spotlight began panning back and forth, trying to pinpoint the riders. In another sixty seconds, they'd be visible, and there was simply nowhere to hide out here. Bolan was considering pulling to a stop and trying to take out the spotlight when another flare lit the sky. Gunfire erupted beneath it.

To Bolan's surprise and relief, whoever was shooting

was aiming for the helicopter and not them. He heard the sharp ping of a round connecting with the chopper's metal frame, then red emergency vehicle lights blazed into life. Tony and Bolan crashed through scrub brush and across the creek, which was more dirt than water. Looking over his shoulder, Bolan watched the chopper veering away to the south once more.

They reined in as they entered the area lit up by the emergency flashers. As the dust settled, Bolan realized they belonged to a lone, old fire truck. Eleanor strutted out from behind it, a rifle slung over her shoulder. The older woman looked supremely confident and proud as she laid eyes on her husband and nodded to Bolan.

Tony climbed out of the saddle and swept his wife into his arms. Bolan glanced away, trying to give them a private moment. "You boys gave me a fright," Eleanor said when the embrace ended. "I was beginning to wonder if I'd have to start traipsing across the Mexican desert to look for you."

Bolan dismounted. "I'm afraid it was my fault. Your husband had to put me back together after he found me, and it took a little doing. Plus, we ended up with extra company."

"I saw that," she said. "I'd say you were lucky that Tony found you, and both of you were lucky to get back alive."

"I'll take luck any time I can get it," Tony said. "Did you bring the trailer?"

She nodded. "Let's load up your horses and get home. A hot meal, a shower and some sleep will have both of you feeling better by sunrise."

"How did you know where we'd be?" Bolan asked, his curiosity piqued. "It's a big desert."

"Tracker," Tony said. "She made me start carrying one on these treks years ago. Told me it was to keep me safe, but I think it was just to make sure I wasn't spending time with any of the local *señoritas* south of the border. They can be downright friendly to a man who's open to that sort of thing."

"He's silly," Eleanor said, taking his arm in hers as he led his horse with the other.

Bolan helped them load up the horses, taking quiet stock of his injuries and what had happened since he'd come down here. He'd failed to be as serious about the situation as he should have been, and he'd failed to keep an ally safe. So far, he'd done nothing to stop the flow of weapons going into Sureno's enterprise. But he was alive, and he had strong, intelligent people on his side.

And as they drove through the darkness toward Tony's little ranch, he realized something else. When he'd arrived in Arizona, this had been just another mission.

Now, it was personal.

11

Rene Sureno despised failure almost as much as he despised being made a fool. The men standing in the courtyard were not *quite* guilty of the latter crime, but that was only because they had tried to rectify their mistakes. Losing the American was an idiotic fuckup, and someone must take the blame and the punishment for it. The three men he had decided were most responsible—the man who should've stopped Cooper in the house, the man who should've locked the gate, and the man flying the helicopter—now hung by their ankles in the courtyard.

They had been flogged senseless, and blood and sweat dripped from their frames. For the moment, they were unconscious. At least that had stopped the screaming. If they lived through the day, Sureno would allow them to be cut down and their injuries treated, but until then they would serve as a graphic reminder of failure to perform to his standards.

He gestured at the three forms, then turned his attention back to his assembled men. "This is what happens to incompetent fools. Tomorrow, you will do better, or I will make certain that you receive the same treatment. Is that understood?"

"Si!" The shout echoed in the courtyard, though every eye was cast downward in respect or fear. For Sureno's current purposes, either one would suffice.

He nodded at Jesus, who dismissed the men, then gave his orders regarding the fate of the other three.

Throughout the event, Isabel had stood in silence next to him, her eyes looking everywhere but at the spectacle of the beatings. When they were finally alone, she turned to him. "Blaming them doesn't solve anything," she said. "The American is gone. I don't know why you hold them responsible."

"Who else was I to blame, Isabel? Those three men failed me, allowing Cooper to get away from the compound, and even in the desert, he found assistance. Is there someone else at fault?"

She shook her head and lowered her gaze to the ground. Sureno grabbed her under the chin.

"Did you have something to do with this, Isabel?" His eyes bored into hers, trying to force any necessary confession. He knew she was weak.

"No! No, Rene! I would never betray you," she said. Her voice was shaking.

Sureno continued to stare at her, then released her chin. "Never forget that you are mine, Isabel. If you were to break my trust, your fate would be far worse than those men. You would beg to die, and I would see to it that you lived."

"I will always be loyal to you, Rene. I only meant that…"

"What?"

"That beating them changes nothing. The American is still gone."

"Yes," he said. "That's true. But beating them wasn't

about changing anything, my soft-hearted one. It was about instilling the discipline necessary for our plans to succeed." He pulled her to his side and kissed the top of her head, as if he were forgiving a child.

"I'm sure you are right," she said from inside the circle of his arms.

"Of course I am." He turned her around and walked with her toward the main house. "You go and rest now. I will come and see you later."

Isabel kissed his cheek, then moved down the hallway, and he went into his office to make the call he'd been putting off for several hours in the hopes they'd get lucky and find Cooper. But luck and time had run out. Sureno sat at his desk and dialed the number that would connect him to Kingston's boss. It rang twice before Mr. Bricker picked up.

"This is a surprise, Rene. You broke him faster than I expected. I guess they don't make operatives like they used to."

Rene sighed. "I did not break him. He escaped."

The silence on the other end of the phone stretched out for what seemed a very long time before the other man spoke again. "How…how could he *possibly* have escaped? You live in a fucking fortress in the desert. Find him, Rene!"

"We tried, Bricker, but he had help on the outside. He was not as alone as you made him out to be, and he reached the border. He's your problem now. I don't think he's stupid enough to come back here."

"There wouldn't *be* a problem if you'd just done your job, Rene. I handed him to you on a silver platter wrapped in a bow, and you couldn't manage to hang on to him."

Irritated, Rene said, "He was *your* man's problem to begin with, Bricker, so I suggest you deal with him. I can always find another supplier."

Another moment passed in silence. "I don't like being threatened, Rene. And I'm the only supplier you'll work with, or I'll put you out of business myself. Got me?"

Rene held his tongue, and Bricker went on. "I'm going to take care of this little problem for you, and then you and I are going to have to revisit our arrangement."

"Fine," Rene said. "I'll look forward to it." He slammed the phone down in the cradle and looked up to see Jesus watching him from the doorway.

"Problem?" he asked.

"Nothing we can't handle," Rene said. "In my experience, if there's a buyer like me, one can always find a seller. When this matter with the American is concluded, we will have to take care of Bricker and find someone less…"

"Of an ass?" he suggested.

"That suffices," Rene said. "Start thinking about how to arrange it."

Jesus nodded. "Consider it done."

THE LINE WENT dead and Bricker hung up the phone. The fucking idiot on the other side of the border was making life far too interesting, and he'd had enough of him to last a lifetime. He picked up the phone again and dialed a number from memory.

"Kingston," a voice answered on the first ring.

"Brett," he said. "We may have to move on Sureno sooner than expected. I'm going to put the team on alert. When we move, it will have to be fast."

"Are you sure that's necessary? I mean, who will we—"

"Let me worry about finding a new buyer, Kingston. This is the border and there's always another cartel in Mexico looking for the kind of items we provide. You just do your part and keep things moving."

"All right, Mr. Bricker. Do you need me to do anything else?"

"Yes," he said. "I want you to start looking for more information on this man, Matt Cooper or Colonel Brandon Stone or whoever the hell he is. He's not just some snoop for DHS. If you find out anything, get it to me immediately."

"Yes, sir," Kingston said. "I can start digging on both names right away."

"Good. That idiot Sureno lost him, and he's back on home turf. We're going to need to find him and take him out of play too."

"That shouldn't be too difficult," Kingston said. "He'll come back to Sierra Vista or run for the hills. Either way, we'll find him."

"Get on it, then," Bricker said, ending the call. He leaned back in his chair. If everything went right, he'd be done with two problems in short order, and he'd be a wealthier man because of it. All in a day's work for a man who'd learned that the best way to serve Uncle Sam was to serve himself first.

12

Bolan swung his legs over the side of Tony and Eleanor's guest bed and stretched. The home-cooked meal and hot shower the night before had done him good, and with a solid rest behind him, he was ready to get back to work. He picked up his handheld, dialing the direct line for Hal Brognola at his office in the Justice Department.

Brognola answered in the middle of the second ring. "Striker, it's good to hear from you."

"You won't feel that way when I'm done speaking," Bolan replied.

"I'd tell you I was surprised, but I'd be lying. Did you run into some trouble?"

Bolan gave Brognola the rundown of the past few days. Brognola listened carefully, not saying anything until Bolan finished his report.

"This sounds much more serious than we'd initially thought," Brognola said. "How in the hell did a bunch of thugs get their hands on so much hardware?"

"I have a few leads, but they're lukewarm at best. I'd like to get some support down here."

"I'm writing it up right now," Brognola said. "What do you need?"

"I need a vehicle that can take on desert terrain, plus

a good field communications and observation package. Also, a new set of weapons would be helpful."

"No problem. I'll send all of that out of Phoenix. It should get to you by midday. Do you need personnel?"

"It's not a horrible idea," Bolan replied. "I've got some local help, but another set of eyes never hurts. Didn't you mention an agent in Phoenix?"

"Nadia Merice. I can have her on a flight first thing, and she can deliver your vehicle and gear at the same time."

"I don't know her, Hal," Bolan said. "Is she any good? I don't want to take a rookie into this mess."

There was a brief pause as he heard Brognola's fingers typing something into the computer. "I've got her profile right here. Portuguese and Spanish heritage, speaks both fluently, and she looks it, so she won't stick out. She's done work for CIA and NSA, and she's field qualified in weapons and hand-to-hand. She can handle herself."

"All right," Bolan said. "Send her along."

"Consider it done. I'll brief the President myself this morning. As soon as I can, I'll start digging around to see what I can scare up in terms of intelligence."

"Thanks for the help, Hal. I appreciate it. Tell Merice to plan on meeting me in Sierra Vista by early afternoon at the latest, and pass along my number, would you?"

"I'll make sure she's got what she needs, Striker. I'll be in touch."

Bolan ended the call, already thinking through the numerous steps it would take to get the wheels in motion. Finding that his clothes had already been washed, dried and set out on the dresser, Bolan dressed then strolled out into the kitchen. Tony and Eleanor were sitting at the table, sipping coffee. The old man was playing a game of solitaire with a deck of cards that was almost as worn as he was. Both of them looked pretty tired, and Bolan knew that he owed the older couple his life.

"Morning," Eleanor said. "I'll get you some hot breakfast."

"Please, sit," Bolan said. "I can manage coffee and toast if you'll just point me in the right direction."

The woman ignored him and shooed him toward the table. "The day I can't make a man his breakfast in my own home is the day they put me in the ground," she said. "You take your coffee with anything?"

"Just attitude," he said, smiling as she brought him a cup.

He watched as she moved around the kitchen, comfortable in her domain. Occasionally, she would make eye contact with Tony or share a smile or a brief touch. Olivia would be missing that for many years to come, if not the rest of her life.

The smell of frying eggs and bacon filled the kitchen, and Eleanor had plates ready for all three of them in record time. They ate in comfortable silence, enjoying the quiet of the day and the stillness before the next battle—whatever it was going to be. When they were finished, Bolan stood and poured himself a second cup of coffee.

"Thank you, Eleanor," he said. "That was delicious. I don't get a lot of home-cooked meals these days."

"You're welcome, Matt. Tony was the same way back in the day."

The old man cocked an eyebrow at his wife. "My day isn't over quite yet," he said, then turned to Bolan. "What's next?"

"First stop is Douglas," he said. "I need to go and see Olivia. Then I'll get a lift over to Sierra Vista."

"We'll go with you," Eleanor said.

Bolan shook his head. "I don't want either of you taking any more risks on my behalf. I'm already indebted to you both."

Eleanor started to argue, but Tony nodded. "He's right, hon. I'll take him. You stay here and mind the home fires."

She gave him a hard stare for a long minute, then sighed and shook her head. "You just see to it that you come back in one piece. You understand me, old man? You're not fifty anymore!"

"Ha!" he laughed. "Neither are you, but you sure do look it!"

They laughed together and Bolan joined in. He couldn't change the fact that Rivers was gone or that his wife and daughter would miss him. But he could make those responsible pay for their crimes. In his line of work, that would have to be enough.

THE SMALL HOUSE that had been so inviting and full of life a few days before was covered in a pall of sadness, yet Olivia was kind enough—strong enough—to smile and pull Bolan into a warm hug.

"I'm so glad you're all right," she said. "I didn't know who else to call, and I figured that if anyone could find you, Tony could. The Border Patrol said they didn't know anything about you. One of them even suggested that maybe you were the one who…"

"Killed Colton?" he finished for her.

She nodded, finding her voice again and fighting off the tears. "I knew that couldn't be true, but they all thought I was hysterical." She started pacing the room. "What happened, Matt?" she asked. "Tell me."

"I'll tell you everything I can," Bolan said. "Let's just sit down and talk through it."

Tony guided her to a chair. "When was the last time you ate something?"

"I…I don't know," she said. "All I can think about is Colton. My mom came and took Katrina out for the day. I haven't been sleeping."

"We're going to fix you right up," Bolan said. "Tony, do you think it would be okay for Eleanor to come down and visit for a spell? Lend Olivia here a hand?"

"I think that would be fine," he said.

"Why don't you go in the kitchen and give her a call?"

"I'll get to it," Tony said, heading in that direction.

Bolan turned back to the young woman. "Olivia, I'm going to find the men responsible for this, I promise you."

"Just tell me what happened," she said.

He described how they were ambushed, making certain to be as general as possible. He saw no point in upsetting her with any graphic details. When he finished, he took her hands in his. "They'll pay in full," he said. "With interest."

"Please take care of yourself. You were already taken by them once." Her eyes were wet with unshed tears. "What happened to Colton is bad enough, and you were trying to help him. I don't want you to get killed, too."

"I won't," he said. "And I feel responsible, Olivia. I can't tell you how sorry I am that Colton died. I should've been more wary of the situation, but it won't happen again. I'll find them and they will be brought to justice."

"Just be careful," she said. "Your death won't change what's happened."

"I always am," he said, looking up as Tony came back into the room carrying a small bowl of soup. "Now eat and then rest. When you wake up, Eleanor will be here and she'll stay with you until things are…"

"Better?" she said, her voice flat. She barked a short, cynical laugh. "I don't think there is any better."

Bolan nodded. "Justice is better," he said. "Eat your soup."

AFTER LEAVING OLIVIA, Bolan and Tony drove in silence to Sierra Vista. En route, Bolan received a text from Brognola confirming that Nadia Merice would meet him as scheduled in the parking lot of the grocery store on Fry Boulevard. He passed the information along to Tony, who indicated that he knew the exact spot.

A short time later, he pulled into the designated parking lot and shut off the engine. When he started to get out of the truck, Bolan put his hand on the old man's arm.

"You need all the help you can get, Matt," Tony said.

Bolan chuckled. "You're right about that, but you've done enough for now."

"You're benching me?" Tony asked.

"No, Tony, I'm not. I've got another job in mind for you and before we talk to Nadia, I want you to know what it is."

"Well, shoot then," he said.

"I want you back in the desert, keeping an eye on Sureno and his crew. I'm going to give you a sat phone, and if you see something worth reporting, you share it with me."

"That sounds an awful lot like the bench," Tony complained. "A lot of sitting and waiting."

Bolan shook his head. "I can't be everywhere at once," he said. "I need someone keeping an eye on things who won't get caught or killed while he's at it. That's you."

"I won't slow you down," Tony said, "if that's what you're thinking. I can still carry my own ruck."

"Tony, you don't have to prove your worth to me. You've already saved my neck once. But I need someone to keep an eye on the ground over there. Have Eleanor stay with Olivia and make sure she's protected—I don't want any of this blowing back on her. She's sacrificed enough. In the meantime, you head back, gear up and get out there. Let me do what I do best."

"What is it you do best?"

"I finish the job," Bolan said.

Tony nodded reluctantly, agreeing to his plan. Bolan watched the parking lot, and a few moments later, a Conquest Knight XV pulled in and came to a stop. It was the kind of luxury SUV used by the incredibly wealthy who needed—or thought they needed—high-end protection. With the right options, it was a vehicle made to drive up to the gates of hell and roll right through them, all while looking and feeling like a Cadillac. A woman climbed out of the driver's side.

Her black hair was cut in a severe, short style that accented her high cheekbones. She couldn't have been more than five feet tall, and that was giving her a bonus for the heel of her knee-high boots. Her loose-fitting shirt billowed in the breeze. She nodded as Bolan climbed out of Tony's truck.

"Nadia Merice?" he asked, moving toward her.

"That's me," she said. "You must be Cooper."

"Got it in one," he said. They studied each other in silence for a long moment.

Tony got out of the truck and headed in their direction. "Who's the geezer?" she asked, a small smile playing at the corners of her mouth.

"Tony Altera," the older man said. "Show some respect, young lady."

Bolan was ready to step in when she burst out laughing. "I thought that might be your name. They still talk about you up in the Phoenix area."

"They?" Bolan asked.

"Federal law enforcement," she said. "Tony here is almost a legend."

"Almost," Tony said. He offered a hand, which she took.

"Good," Bolan said. "Now that we're all introduced, let's get to work, yes?"

"Sounds fine," she said. "What's the plan?"

"Tony here is going to head back out to the desert and do what he does best—which is being invisible. Do you have a sat phone in the Knight?"

She nodded.

"Give him one, and program it with our numbers. As soon as she's done, Tony, you head out."

"What about you?" she asked as Bolan started in the direction of the store.

"I'm going to buy a cup of coffee and a can of bug spray."

"Bug spray?" she asked.

"Yeah, for when we start poking the hornet's nest."

13

After watching Tony drive off, Bolan and Merice headed for the car rental company a few blocks away. "What's wrong with my truck?" she asked.

"It stands out like a sore thumb," Bolan said. "But mostly, we're going to need to split up at some point, so it's best to have two vehicles."

They picked up a nondescript Mercury sedan, then Bolan gave Merice instructions to enter the base and watch the warehouse. If Kingston left by himself, she was to follow him and get in touch by radio if she needed help. If he left with someone else, she'd find Bolan outside the gate, and they'd adjust the plan.

There was no need for Bolan himself to reenter Fort Huachuca. Instead, he simply parked his vehicle in the hotel lot across the street and waited. The gate logs showed that Hansen, Kingston's assistant, came and went though the main gate, and it was nearing the end of the day.

Bolan didn't want to confront Hansen on post; he wanted to do it somewhere much more private. Brognola felt that Hansen was the most likely culprit, and Bolan agreed—the man had access to the altered bills of lading and inventory files. Their plan was basic enough:

Brognola let word trickle down that someone in Kingston's warehouse was moving weapons illegally and making backdoor deals. Hansen would hear about it, and he'd be nervous. Nervous enough, Bolan hoped, that he'd make a mistake—or at least be more willing to cooperate when they had their chat.

Bolan watched the main gate and sure enough, at 4:30—a full half-hour before he usually left— Hansen drove out and turned north on Highway 90. He was driving a dark blue Ford Taurus that had seen better days. If he was involved in the weapons smuggling, he certainly wasn't spending his money on his car. Bolan pulled out of the parking lot and onto the highway, giving his target plenty of room. This was no time to get into a car chase; Bolan wanted to see where he went to ground.

Hansen stayed the course for a solid fifteen minutes. He slowed down at a wide spot in the road called Huachuca City, and on its northern outskirts, he turned right. Realizing he was entering a small trailer park, Bolan slowed even more. Roads tended to be narrow and short in trailer parks, and it wouldn't do to be seen. No other roads were in sight, so Hansen would be parked somewhere inside.

Bolan waited ten minutes, then pulled into the trailer park. It was only four streets wide, with a handful of old, single-wide trailers. Most of them had been bleached white or gray by the desert sun. The Taurus was parked at the end of the street farthest from the entrance. Pleased by the convenience of the location, Bolan stopped two trailers away and shut off the engine.

Stepping into the evening, Bolan strolled down the street. There were no signs of children in the area, and by the looks of it, this was a place where base personnel crashed for a short time until they could find something better—like a room in the lobby of hell. Cracked window glass, vehicles with missing tires, and paltry, dying lawns made up of weeds more than anything else were the hallmarks of the landscape. Most of the trailers had window air-conditioning units running full-blast in an attempt to keep the poorly insulated trailers even vaguely cool. No one was outside and no one peered through their windows to see who the stranger walking down the street might be.

Bolan reached the trailer where Hansen had parked and slipped quietly up the concrete steps to the door, pausing to listen. He heard movement and suspected that Hansen was alone. Now was as good a time as any. He turned the knob and opened the door quickly, stepping inside with his weapon drawn. The tiny living room, filled with dirty dishes and ratty newspapers, was empty. The sounds were coming from the back of the trailer, and now that Bolan was inside, it was easy to identify them.

Hansen was digging through drawers and packing. In a hurry. Bolan took a silent seat on the arm of the couch and waited. Several minutes later, the man came down the hallway holding a large duffel bag in one arm and a laptop case in the other. He didn't see Bolan until he was halfway into the kitchen.

"Going somewhere, Hansen?" Bolan asked, casually pointing the Desert Eagle in his direction. "Vacation down in old Mexico, perhaps?"

Hansen paled, then dropped the bags, clawing desperately for his back. The Executioner was on him far too fast for the move to be effective. Bolan slammed the butt of the Eagle into Hansen's forehead. As Hansen staggered, bleeding from the easily split skin, Bolan spun him around and removed the small .32 caliber pistol from his waistband. "Take a seat, Hansen," he said, shoving him toward the couch. "We need to talk."

"I don't know anything."

"That's interesting. I haven't asked you anything… yet. Why don't you tell me what it is you think you don't know?"

"But…I mean…I don't know anything about anything, and I don't know why you're here. This is a violation of my civil rights. I want to talk to my lawyer."

"Well, there's a problem with that, Mr. Hansen. I'm not here. Officially, I was never here."

"There are records. If something happens to me, they'll see you were on base the other day and they'll want to ask you questions."

"You're acting like I've already killed you," Bolan said.

"Are you going to kill me?"

"Not yet."

"Yet?"

"It all depends on you and how honest I think you're being. If you're a waste of my time, then things won't go as well as they will if you cooperate."

"But…what do you want to know?"

"I want to know about the weapons being smuggled out of your warehouse and into Mexico."

"Weapons? I don't know—"

Bolan planted his boot into Hansen's chest, cutting off his words. He wriggled, trying to catch his breath as he sank deeper into the couch. His face turned splotchy red before Bolan eased up.

"Let me tell you how this is going to go, Hansen. The time for playing games is finished, and I'm out of patience. Now tell me about the weapons before I have to get creative."

"I can't tell you—he'll kill me."

"Who will kill you?"

"I don't know his name! I just do the paperwork!"

"I don't believe you."

Bolan began applying the pressure again. "Is it Kingston?" he asked, aiming the Desert Eagle at Hansen's forehead. "Give me the name and the details, Hansen, or die protecting someone who wouldn't lift a finger to save your hide."

"Bricker!" he screeched. "That's all I know. His name is Mr. Bricker."

Bolan released the pressure on his chest. "That's a good start," he said, sitting back down. "Now, tell me the rest."

UNTIL THAT MORNING, Nadia Merice had never heard of Matt Cooper, but when Hal Brognola called and said he wanted her to go down to Sierra Vista and do whatever Cooper said needed doing, she'd agreed. In fact, she'd jumped at the chance to get involved.

Sitting in her SUV and watching the warehouse from a block away, she saw Kingston leave by the front and get into a car. He was moving quickly, and she let him head for the gate before she put the transmission in drive and followed discreetly. Cooper was right about one thing—the Conquest was hardly inconspicuous. Still, Brognola had said she needed to bring a vehicle that could take on the terrain, and this one could do that and more.

Kingston went into Sierra Vista out of the gate, heading down the main road. She followed along, taking her time. There wasn't enough traffic that he would be able to easily lose her. He went past a strip mall and a steak-house, then drove for another half mile before turning into a treelined driveway. The corner lot was fenced off, and Merice took the turn alongside the property. She pulled to a stop when she spotted his vehicle parked in front of a ranch-style adobe house.

Merice removed a set of Bushnell PowerView binoculars from the console, then trained them on the vehicle. Kingston had parked next to a large Ford Expedition, and two more SUVs sat between them and the garage. She counted six men besides Kingston, one of whom was speaking animatedly with him. Although she could listen in—she had a nice electronic earpiece in the comm kit in the back—another approach might be more valuable in the long run. She put the binoculars away, then checked her appearance in the mirror. She put the SUV back in gear, then turned around, drove the short distance to the driveway and pulled right in, ignoring the large sign that read No Trespassing.

She saw the group of men stop talking. They all moved in unison, like a military unit, and by the look of these men, all of them were prior service, if not active. She rolled the Conquest to a stop behind Kingston's car and got out, lugging her purse and faking a near-trip as she climbed down from the driver's seat.

"Hi!" she said, waving to the men, who stared at her as though she'd just dropped in from outer space. "Sorry to bother you. Can you help me?" She kept walking until she was standing right next to Kingston and the other man.

Kingston's features softened. "Sure," he said, his eyes resting on her chest. "What can we do for you?"

She giggled. "I'm a little lost," she said. "I came down

to have lunch with my friend Kimmy—do you know her?"

When he shook his head, she giggled again. "It's such a small town, I thought everyone knew everyone. Anyway, we had a little wine at lunch and when I left, I got turned around, and I've been driving in circles ever since!"

"Get rid of her," the man Kingston had been talking to growled under his breath.

"Relax," he said. "Where is it you're trying to go?"

"Home!" she said, spinning in a lazy circle in the direction of the road.

"And where is home?"

"Back to Scottsdale, silly," she said.

"You've been driving around here looking for Scottsdale?" he asked, incredulous. "For how long?"

"Oh, well…" She looked at her watch. "Can you keep a secret?"

"Sure," he said, amused. "What's your secret?"

"I might have had more than a little wine at lunch and then I might have stopped after I got lost at that bar down the road to have a…refresher."

"It sure sounds like it," he said. "Just take a left out of the driveway, and that's Highway 90. Follow it north—that will be on your right—and you'll get back to the interstate in no time."

"Really?" she asked, stumbling a bit toward him and dropping her purse. "I'm so sorry!"

"Oh for God's sake," the other man said, stomping toward the garage.

As Merice scrambled to pick up her purse, she slipped the tracker under the bumper of the nearest truck. "I can be such a klutz sometimes!" she added, getting back up with her purse firmly secured to her shoulder.

"It's okay," he said. "We've got some work to do here. You know where you're going now?"

"Yes, sir," she said. "Out the driveway, left, then go north."

"Right," he said. "Correct, I mean. And take my advice—don't stop at any more bars along the way."

"That's good advice," she said. "If my husband knew I was driving his truck like this, he'd kill me!"

"Then I wouldn't tell him," Kingston replied. "You have a nice day, now."

She walked back to the Conquest, staggering slightly then righting herself before getting in. "Thank you so much!" she called, waving once more.

"Anytime," he said.

Merice backed out of the driveway and turned left. Whatever they'd been talking about, she suspected that what mattered more was where they went. She drove back into town and found the large parking lot where she'd agreed to meet up with Cooper. It was time to bring him up to speed.

14

Agent Merice pulled into the parking lot, and Bolan watched her get out of the vehicle that would draw looks in a city as large as Los Angeles, let alone a small place like Sierra Vista. Still, he couldn't help but smile as she strutted his way. She was all sass and style in a tiny package, but that was only a piece of her allure. Brognola had sent him a brief and her file was a good read. Proficient in undercover work, she'd used her looks to her advantage, but she was just as capable in a fight.

"Were you able to get anything out of Hansen?" she asked, leaning casually against the hood of his car.

"He was pretty cooperative when I threatened his life," he said. "The guy running the show is named Bricker. He was a Marine, Force Recon, before being dishonorably discharged for reasons unknown. Now, he's got quite an operation smuggling weapons into Mexico. I've got Brognola working on tracking him down."

"He must have been the guy Kingston was with when I followed him."

"Oh?" Bolan asked.

"Yeah, I tracked him to a house on the outskirts of town. He met up with a handful of men there, and one of them—a crew cut with a cranky attitude—seemed like he was in charge."

"Interesting."

"The house doesn't look like much more than a staging area and a crash pad. Several trucks were there and at least five other mercs that I saw. Bricker is the chief, but Kingston is in it up to his eyebrows."

"How close did you get?"

"Close enough to put a tracker on one of the trucks."

"That's pretty close," he said.

She slid her sunglasses down and grinned. "I wouldn't say it was an Oscar-worthy performance, but I do a fantastic half-bombed rich-girl-lost."

Bolan smiled back. He liked her. Despite his preference for working on his own, he'd learned that a good agent could be worth his or her weight in gold. In her case, maybe a bit more. He was about to say so when his phone rang. The ID showed it was Brognola, and he answered. "Go ahead, Hal."

"Striker, we have a new complication."

"I'd be lying if I said I was surprised," he quipped.

"This one may be more complicated than usual. They finished the audit of Kingston's warehouse, and like we suspected, a lot of weapons and ammunition are missing. Looking at the paper trail, it started small, but they got greedy. Some of it was as recent as a couple days ago, and it appears that Kingston was diverting some things into a hidden warehouse. If they haven't moved it already, they will soon, and he has to know that the ATF and Army CID are right on his ass."

"What kinds of weapons have been taken?"

"Mostly assault rifles and handguns, plus some field anti-tank weapons like the Javelin. They also managed to land a large shipment of armor-piercing rounds for the rifles. Considering the problems the Justice Department has had with Operation Fast and Furious, the ATF wants this stuff found *before* it gets to Mexico. They'll be going in force to take his warehouse on the base tonight, but you've got to find the rest of it."

"We've got a tracker on one of the trucks they're using," he said. "Merice and I will follow it and see if it leads us to the rest of the weapons."

"Watch yourselves out there, Striker. I've got a feeling this is a lot bigger than we even know about yet. If we can stop them now, Colton Rivers's life won't have been lost in vain. If those weapons get loose in Mexico, a lot of people are going to die."

"We'll get them," Bolan said.

"Good luck, Striker." Brognola ended the call.

Bolan put down the phone and Merice tapped him on the shoulder. She showed him her handheld. A red dot on the screen was heading due east. "That truck is on the move," she said.

"We'll leave my vehicle here," Bolan said.

"I thought my truck was too obvious," Merice said dryly.

"We'll have to risk recognition," Bolan responded. "They're probably going off-road somewhere, and the Conquest can handle the terrain. Let's see what rabbit hole this takes us down."

The GPS took them northeast out of Sierra Vista, following the two-lane blacktop of East Charleston Road. Based on the tracking dot, Bolan estimated they were about ten minutes behind the truck. When the red dot reached Tombstone, it turned northwest on Highway 80.

Shortly thereafter, the blip disappeared from the main roads. The truck had gone into the mountains.

"That's near the Sheepshead Dome," Merice said. "Part of the Dragoon Mountains."

Bolan looked at the overlay on her handheld. "You know the area?"

She nodded. "I've done some hiking near there. It's rough country, and there are a lot of caves."

"Let's see what we can find," he said, guiding her SUV to the last place they'd seen the tracker dot. "My guess is they're using GPS jammers wherever they're holing up. In this case, the lack of signal is actually a clue to their whereabouts."

"Makes sense," Merice said. "There's a little public park and historical marker about a mile up the road. We can cut over from there."

Bolan followed her directions, then turned in on the dirt track she indicated. It made the road to Tony's house look like a well-kept interstate, but the Conquest handled it with ease. He guided the vehicle to a large series of boulders that could give them some cover and parked.

They climbed out of the SUV and made their way past the boulders and closer to the bottom of the hillside.

Using her binoculars, Merice whistled softly. "Take a look at that," she said, pointing and handing them to Bolan.

Through the field glasses, he saw the slightest glint of sun shining off something metal. "Could be anything," he said. "But it's the best lead we've got. Let's go in for a closer look."

THEY RETURNED TO the SUV and checked the position of the device against the satellite feed. "It looks like we can cut back down a bit, then up and across the ridgetop," Nadia said.

"Let's go hunting," Bolan replied, getting back into the truck. "You drive."

"I was wondering how long it was going to take for you to give me a turn," she said, sliding behind the wheel and turning over the turbo diesel engine. "Thought maybe you were some kind of driving chauvinist."

Bolan chuckled. "Not at all. With those tiny legs of yours, I figured you could do with a rest."

"Oh, you are funny," she said, pulling the Conquest out and guiding it back down the road a distance, then cutting upward, finding paths through the rigorous mountain terrain that only a goat might know about. They reached the top of the ridgeline, then doubled back toward where they suspected Bricker had set up shop. In the distance, Bolan spotted several mine tailings and remembered Tony using the old dynamite to help their escape.

"I have an idea," he said. "Do you think the truck can make it to bottom of this ravine and then up onto that hill? I think they've hidden something in that set of caves over there."

"Yeah, this baby can get just about anywhere."

They crept across the ravine, using the turbo booster to climb the last ridge. Rather than get out and lie on their bellies to scope the area, they sat in the air-conditioned Conquest and scanned the hillside using the truck's camera and listening devices.

"I could get used to doing surveillance this way," Bolan said.

"It beats the hell out of lying in the mud or the snow," Merice agreed.

The camera began taking pictures and they zoomed in on their target with the long-range telephoto lens. The caves below had long ago expanded to accommodate the old mining town in the valley. At one time, they might have been used to store equipment or even to serve as a shelter for the teams of men who worked in the mountains. Now, Bolan and Merice could just see the back ends of trucks parked inside and even spotted crates being moved around. From the valley floor, these caves would be invisible. A thin dirt track led to them, and Bolan spotted two men guarding the pathway, no doubt in place to discourage anyone thinking about taking a hike in the immediate area.

"Well, I'd say we found their storage warehouse," Merice said.

"Looks like it," he replied.

"Cooper, how do you suppose they're getting from here down to south of Tombstone where Border Patrol spotted them?"

"This whole area is damn empty," he said, shrugging. "My best guess is that they go almost completely off road from here, waiting until there's so little traffic that getting noticed is rare."

She nodded. "So, now what do you want to do?"

Bolan studied the situation once more. "We'll wait for dark, then go in, unless the trucks start to move out before then."

"What about Bricker and Kingston?" she asked.

"If they leave, we'll let them go—for now," he decided. "Stopping the weapons is more important."

"That's a long wait," Merice said, turning in her seat and reaching into the humidor behind her. She pulled out two cigars, Nicaraguan by their look and smell.

Bolan raised an eyebrow.

"What?" she asked. "If I have to sit and wait for night-fall, I might as well pass the time pleasantly, and my guess is you're not much of a small talker." She wiggled a cigar in front of Bolan. He ignored it, and she eventually pulled it away.

"Fine," she said. "More for me."

"I'm not much for small talk," Bolan said. "But I won't even remember how to do real surveillance after this mission."

She laughed, lighting her cigar. "You don't strike me as a man who forgets much of anything."

Bolan looked once more at the caves, then nodded slightly. "You'd be right about that. I've got a long memory."

15

The daylight hours ticked by as Bolan and Merice waited, watching the cave complex where Bricker was storing the weapons and ammunition. It was nearing dusk when he finally appeared along with two men, Kingston trailing in their wake.

"Here we go," Bolan said. "You've got the electronic ear situated?"

"Yep, and the gain is cranked. There isn't enough interference out here to present a problem, so we should be able to hear them fine." Merice powered it up.

"Are you sure you want to do it this way?" Kingston was asking his boss. "We've gone to a lot of work to set all this up…"

"Sureno is a liability now, and I don't like liabilities," Bricker said. "If he and his roving band of moronic mercenaries hadn't attacked that Border Patrol team, no one would have had the slightest clue what we were doing."

"He said that his man Jesus felt like there wasn't any choice."

"Bullshit," Bricker snarled. "Salazar is a blood-thirsty killer of the first order, and he was testing his muscles. I heard about some of his exploits in the Middle East and Africa. He was a favorite of the warlords looking to tune up their tribesmen."

"So, where does that leave us?" Kingston whined. "Just shit out of luck?"

"Sureno may not know or care about which weapons are killing which people in Mexico, but here in the States, the government gets kinda picky about it. He's sloppy, and cutting him loose is no big loss. I already have a deal ready to set up a little farther south. That will keep things on *that* side of the border and our asses out of the fire."

"Are we really going to take it all back?"

"How you were ever in the Special Forces is a mystery to me," Bricker said, disgust lacing his tone. "Look, the investigation here is going to shut things down for awhile. We take the stash Sureno's sitting on, plus what we have in inventory, and sell it down in central Mexico. With all of that, we can hit the beach on the gulf and live like kings."

This news seems to brighten Kingston's mood considerably. "So, what's the plan?"

"I'm sending a team out with this truck. It will look like it's loaded, but we'll keep most of the stuff stored in these caves for now. They'll go down to Sureno's compound and take him out while you and I finish our business up here. Now quit whining and get the damn truck loaded with those skeleton crates."

Kingston turned and moved back into the cave, shouting orders, while Bricker stayed by the truck and gave the men loading it instructions to make it look good. When they were finished, his team got into the truck while Bricker and Kingston headed for their personal vehicle. Only a handful of men remained on the scene.

Bolan dialed Brognola, leaving his phone on speaker.

"What do you have, Striker?" he asked as soon as he picked up the line.

"You're on speaker with me and Merice," he said. "What we have is a cave full of weapons and a small group of guards, while a truck just pulled out and headed south. Seems like Bricker has decided it's time to pull up stakes. He's sending a hit crew down to take out Sureno."

"Do they have more weapons in the truck?"

"Probably a few," Merice said. "But it sounded like they just wanted it to look good enough to get close to Sureno."

"Did Bricker go with them? Can you hit it before they get on the road?"

"The odds would not be in our favor," Bolan said. "He's got a well-armed team on it. Bricker and Kingston left in their own vehicle, so my guess is that they're headed back into Sierra Vista to close up shop. Give the ATF our location. By the time they get here, we'll have this area locked down tight."

"They've already secured Kingston's warehouse at Fort Huachuca," Brognola said. "They'll post men there in case he comes back."

"Well, we'd best get to it," Bolan said. "Tell the ATF not to come rolling in here, guns blazing."

"I will. You and Merice just secure those weapons. We'll deal with Bricker later."

"Yes, sir," Merice said.

"Yes, *sir?*" Bolan asked as he ended the call. "This isn't the Army, you know."

"A little respect goes a long way, *Striker,*" she said. "What kind of a nickname is that?"

"A nicer one than the other names people call me," he said.

"I can imagine that people call you all kinds of things," she said. "Ready to get to work?"

Bolan looked at Merice. "I am. Do you think you can tear yourself away from the lap of luxury here to go and take down some bad guys?"

"I'm not thrilled about it," she said, patting the seat. "This is practically an easy chair."

"Come on," Bolan said. "Let's gear up and see if you're everything your file makes you out to be."

"Oh, I'm more than a file," she said, climbing out of the vehicle.

"I hope so," he said.

THE SUN DROPPED below the mountains and left the rugged path up to the cave in shadows. Using night vision goggles, Bolan had spotted two men guarding the path itself and another three moving around inside the cave. It seemed like a safe bet that there were at least a couple more men farther in.

He spoke softly, the mike connected to his earpiece strong enough to pick up even a whisper. "Merice, are you in position?"

"Ready when you are," she said from her post among the rocks. "I'd appreciate it if you didn't get me killed with this plan."

"You'll be fine," he said. "Just remember to turn left when you get to them and keep it quiet."

"Understood," she said. "Moving now."

"Go," he said, watching the path through the scope of the Tactical Operations Tango 51 sniper rifle. Merice had brought it along in the gear, and with a suppressor attached, chambered for .308, it was perfect for quietly removing guards and anyone else he needed to put in the crosshairs. The reputation of the gun as deadly accurate and its preferred use by SWAT teams in major cities told him that at least his diminutive partner wasn't clueless when it came to weapon selection.

He watched as she walked calmly up the path, and then he moved the scope so he could see the guards' reactions. They were in very official-looking uniforms and were already pointing to the large no-trespassing sign near their post. Nadia cheerfully ignored them until she was close.

Through her earpiece, he could hear the conversation with ease.

"Ma'am, this is a no trespassing area. Government property. You're going to have to turn back."

"Ohh…" she said. "I'm sorry. I just got a bit turned around while I was hiking."

"It happens out here. Every rock looks the same," he said.

"I…I don't suppose one of you could give me a lift back to my car?" she asked. "It's at that park?" She pointed vaguely into the distance.

"Sorry, ma'am," the closest guard said. "We're not allowed to leave."

"You can say that again," she said, moving to her left with stunning speed and drawing a flashing weapon from behind her back.

Bolan fired once, hitting the guard she'd been talking to in the heart. The shot was quiet enough that it was unlikely to have been heard in the cave. He adjusted the scope, but Nadia had done her part. The guard to her left was also dying, his throat cut from ear-to-ear in one smooth motion. He clutched at his gushing throat, apparently wanting to find words, air, anything, but nothing came except crimson, frothy bubbles. He spasmed once, then died.

She turned to where Bolan was positioned among the rocks and offered a smile and a wave, then began dragging the bodies off the road.

By the time he'd crossed the hundred yards to Merice, the bodies were no longer in sight and full dark was upon them. The cave was dimly lit from within, but Bolan doubted it would be bright enough to be seen from Tombstone, given the brightness and direction. He checked his watch.

"I figure the ATF will be here within fifteen minutes," he said. "There's three more at the entrance to the cave, plus however many are left inside."

"Well, let's go up there and take them out," she said, lithely moving up the road. She moved like a panther and Bolan watched appreciatively, as he broke into a light jog to catch up.

"How do you want to do this?" she asked. They'd stopped about twenty-five yards from the cave, hidden behind a cluster of boulders. The three men were positioned at the cave mouth, casually smoking cigarettes at the front end of one of the trucks.

"I took a hard look at the entrance before we lost the light. I think we can come at them from both sides," Bolan said. "If you want to circle left, I'll go right, and we can coordinate our attack on the center."

He moved around the boulders, keeping a low profile. The guards seemed to be paying no serious attention to the environment and it only took a few minutes for

Bolan to get in place. He gave Merice another sixty seconds, then keyed his comm. "Are you ready?" he asked.

"I've been waiting for you," she said. "Let's do this."

"Go when I fire," he said. "And don't forget—"

Merice's first shot cut him off, and he couldn't help but grin. He rose from behind his cover and sighted on the closest man, squeezing off a shot from the Desert Eagle. It boomed like a cannon off the rocks and he was dead before he hit the ground, the nearly dinner-plate-sized exit wound spattering the truck with gore.

The third man dove beneath the front end of the truck, and both Merice's and Bolan's shots missed. "Close in," he said. "And watch for stragglers."

He jogged toward the cave entrance, keeping the rock face on his right. On the far side, he saw Merice flicker into view in his goggles, then disappear alongside the truck. In the back of the cave, confused shouts told him there were at least a couple more men, wondering about the fate of their comrades.

Bolan knelt down and peered beneath the truck, but the guard was gone. He'd obviously crawled further into the cave. "Careful," he said. "The third one is in here somewhere, and there are more in the back."

"You're violating the Rules of Oblivion," she said, her voice a breathy whisper in his ear.

He slipped inside the cave, considered asking about the Rules of Oblivion and decided against it, then moved silently between two trucks. He watched the shadows for signs of movement. Weapons crates were stacked along the walls—enough to support a small army—and he noted plenty of places to hide.

Bolan thought he heard the scrape of a foot on stone

and stopped, easing into a wheel well. Suddenly, he saw one of the guards creep forward from between the rows of crates, an M16 held firmly in his hands.

16

Even in the confined space of the cave, when the enemy already knew he was present, Bolan hesitated to use the Desert Eagle. The sound might allow another man to pinpoint his position, and at the moment, he and Merice had the advantage. He put the gun back into the holster and drew a KA-BAR knife from the sheath in his boot.

The guard stepped closer, taking his time, and the Executioner waited with the patience of a stone. There was no need to rush, as the man would be close enough to take out in two, maybe three, more steps. Bolan kept still, his lungs barely taking in oxygen as the man took one step, then another. A slight scratching sound came from behind him and his eyes went wide. The guard spun, trying to bring the rifle into play.

Catlike, Bolan stepped up behind him, jamming his blade into the back of the man's knee and hamstringing him neatly. He toppled and then fell dead to the floor, Merice's own knife buried hilt-deep in his throat.

"I had this one taken care of," Bolan hissed. "There are others in the back."

Her eyebrows quirked upward. "It seemed like you had it all under control, what with the hiding in the wheel well and all."

"You're not funny," he said. "Let's just finish this."

"Brognola told me you didn't have much of a sense of humor."

Bolan sighed heavily, thought about saying more, then shook his head. He stepped over the dead guard and began moving through the cavern once more, Merice flitting from shadow to shadow ahead of him. They reached a barricade of ammunitions and weapons crates, and Bolan assumed the last guards—two or three of them, judging by what he'd heard earlier—were holed up behind it.

Outside, the sound of chopper blades cutting the night air was a welcome noise. The ATF would be on the ground in moments. Bolan and Merice took up covered positions, then he called out, "Federal agents! Throw your weapons down and come out of there with your hands up!"

They could both hear the hurried whispers of the guards, then three rifles and a couple of handguns were tossed over the barricade. "We're coming out!" a voice shouted. "Don't shoot!"

The three men moved cautiously out of their shelter, their hands raised high. Outside the cave, the chopper was landing and Bolan could hear ATF agents moving into the area. He stepped out from behind his own cover, keeping the Desert Eagle trained on the three men. "On the ground!" he ordered. "Now!"

They did as he said, and Bolan nodded to the ATF men as they closed in, identifying himself as Colonel Brandon Stone. They rushed forward, putting cuffs on the men. "We about done here?" Merice asked Bolan.

"Yeah," he said, "we're about done."

On a flimsy card table by the barricade, a cheap rotary phone rang. Bolan stepped away to answer it, spoke quietly for a moment, then hung it up.

"You were expecting a call?" she asked.

He chuckled softly. "No, but it's only polite to answer a ringing phone."

She shook her head. "So, what's next?"

"We go after Bricker and Kingston, and on the way, you explain the Rules of Oblivion."

"I can't," she said, slipping the sling of her rifle over a shoulder and following him as he moved back toward the cave entrance.

"Can't? Why not?"

"I'd be violating one of the rules if I did," she said.

"I'm speechless with surprise," Bolan quipped. "Let's go."

FOR MEN LIKE Bricker, there were days when he didn't want to get out of bed and days when battles made time stand still and everything was awash in blood and fire. Then were days like this one, where he longed for either one of those alternatives. The ATF had a squad of men posted at the gate of Fort Huachuca, and he had no doubt they were looking for him.

Kingston and Bricker drove the perimeter of the fort and watched as the ATF confiscated the weapons that were to be their cash crop. The agents were going over every crate with meticulous precision, taking notes on their clipboards, and with each tick of a pen Bricker could see the dollar bills being taken away. He seethed at the notion that it was all so close, more money than he'd ever need, yet he'd missed the mark.

He picked up the phone and dialed the camp out by Tombstone. They would need to secure the weapons and get them moved to a safer location until he could arrange for their final transport. The phone rang four times before it was answered, a gruff voice that snapped, "Yeah."

"Gregor, what the hell took so long?"

"This isn't Gregor."

"Who is this?"

"I think you know who this is. Your weapons are gone, Bricker. I'm coming for you next."

Bricker hit the END button on his cell phone and threw it on the floor. "Sonofa... Fuck!" he yelled, pounding the dash.

"What is it? What's happened?" Kingston asked.

"That damn agent, Stone or Cooper or whoever he is, they've hit the caves. Everything there is lost."

"Oh, God. We've got to get out of here."

"We will, but we're going to make one stop first," Bricker said.

"Stop? What stop? We need to leave. *Now!*"

"Calm down. We're going to leave, but we need some leverage."

"How are we going to get that?"

"You'll see," he said. It was always good to have a backup plan.

THE DRIVE SOUTH from Tombstone wasn't long, but the hours were beginning to take their toll. Bolan shook off the fatigue, stuffing it into a place in his mind where it would have to wait for later, and took a long drink of water. The fight was just starting, and he knew he needed to be prepared for the battle.

His handheld rang. Tony was on the line.

"These boys are getting busy down here," Tony said.

"What do you mean?" Bolan asked.

"I mean they look like they're hunkering down for an all-out war. You're not going to be able to get within fifty feet without taking heavy fire. They're settling in for a long battle—looks like they know you're coming."

"I can't imagine they're going to all of that trouble for me," Bolan said.

"I'm sure you got under their skin, but these boys look like they're getting ready for the four horsemen themselves to come riding in."

"Okay, stay on them, but if it starts getting too hot, you get your tail out of there."

"Don't worry. I've lived this long and I've no intention of sticking my neck out just to have it chopped off. I'll stay as long as I can."

"Thanks, Tony."

RENE STOOD IN his office, outlining the duties of his sentries with Jesus, who was bent over a map of the compound. There'd been too many surprises and he wasn't going to let any new complications get in the way. He knew every inch of his hacienda, and he'd defend what was his to his last breath.

He worked alongside Jesus, ignoring the ringing phone. He knew who it was, and he wanted him to sweat. The gringos weren't managing their own problems, and he was getting sick of cleaning up their mess. Bricker was a good asset, but sometimes you needed to cut your losses. With the American operative in the mix, the stakes were getting too high. The third time the phone started to ring, he picked it up.

"Hello."

"Where the hell have you been?" Bricker yelled.

"I've been right here the whole time, but I don't answer to you, my friend. You work for me, remember?"

Jesus straightened up and watched Rene as he spoke. Rene maintained his casual pose but wanted to slam the phone down on Bricker.

"I don't work for you, Rene, but we do have a business arrangement. Look, we're coming your way and I have one last delivery for you, but then I'm out of business for a while."

"Why? What happened?"

"The ATF is what happened. The damn prisoner that you let escape has *happened* and half my damn inventory is in the hands of the feds. We're coming your way. We have to make a new deal."

Rene paused and looked down at the plans for his defenses before he responded.

"Sure, my friend. You come here and we'll work everything out."

Rene smiled as he hung up the phone and tossed it to Jesus.

"We need to finish all of our preparations right away. We have guests coming and we want to be ready."

THE GUARDHOUSE AT the gates of Fort Huachuca was normally manned by two soldiers, but as Bricker and Kingston watched from the parking lot of the hotel across the street, they could see four—two of them ATF agents. The main gate wasn't an option, but Bricker hadn't really believed it would be. He picked up the two-way radio from the console and keyed the mike.

"Alpha team, what's your position?"

"Twenty meters from the fence line, Eagle," came the reply. "And closing."

"Bravo team?" Bricker asked.

"We're in position," his man said, "holding."

"Now what?" asked Kingston. The nervous pitch in his voice sounded so much like a dog whining for a bone that it was all Bricker could do not to backhand him across the face. The man was a pathetic excuse for a soldier of any kind.

"Now we wait," he finally replied. "And when the work is done, we go."

"If we pull this off," Kingston said.

Bricker ignored him. "Alpha team, initiate contact as soon as you reach the fence line," he said into the radio.

"Roger that, Eagle," the man replied.

Bricker knew that each five-man team would do its job—it's what they'd trained for their entire lives—and Fort Huachuca was hardly a hotbed of danger. The perimeter guards were spaced out too far apart to repel a serious assault and the ATF was already guarding his warehouse. He didn't need to check to confirm that at this very moment, a dozen or more agents were inside it, counting his inventory and discovering that he'd been selling weapons for months. The question that would be on their minds was where the weapons had gone. They wouldn't expect an attack.

"Initiating contact," the radio squawked. "Line open."

Bricker listened as Alpha team began cutting through the fence, setting off alarms and drawing perimeter guards from all over the base. The sound of periodic gunfire started up as the team peeled open the fence and then fell back into the desert scrub.

"Hold position, Alpha team," Bricker ordered. "And keep firing."

"Acknowledged, Eagle," said the squad leader.

"Bravo team," he said, "move in."

Six hundred meters away, Bravo team waited and watched as the guards covering the fence in their area ran toward the ongoing firefight with Alpha team. As soon as it was clear, they moved forward, cutting through the fence with ease. No additional alarm sounded for this secondary breach. The guards were supposed to hold their positions in circumstances like this, but Bricker knew better. No soldier, not even a part-time National Guardsman just serving his weekend, would ignore gunfire on the fence.

"Bravo team, in position and in the interior," came the report.

Bricker nodded, pleased. The plan was working as he'd expected. "Alpha team," he ordered, "pull back fifty meters and continue to draw fire."

"It's working," Kingston said from the passenger seat.

"We haven't done anything yet," he replied.

Alpha team acknowledged the command, and Bricker heard the leader relay the order to his squad. The sound of running feet, interspersed with assault rifle fire, punctuated the night. The guards at the shack lowered the arm of the gate and closed the fence. The ATF agents scanned the road, waiting for any sign of a frontal assault. As far as Bricker was concerned, they could wait all night.

"Bravo team in ready position," said the voice from the radio. "Infrared shows ten agents in the warehouse, plus two at the door. All on alert."

Bricker considered it, then shrugged. The odds weren't great, but his men were soldiers. "Engage," he ordered.

"Acknowledged, Eagle," came the whispered reply. "Stand by."

The line went dead. All he could do now was wait and hope that his plan would work. If it did, all the losses would be recovered and he'd have his money and revenge on Cooper or Stone or whatever the hell the man's name was. Not even he would be immune to chemical weapons.

In the far distance, he saw the sky light up with a flare. Alpha team was doing a fine job keeping the guards busy. If all went well, Bravo team would have his weapons in hand within five minutes, the ATF would be short twelve more agents and Bricker would be on his way to the border, ready to make a killing. Literally and figuratively.

"It's working, isn't it?" Kingston said again. "When will we know?"

Another flare lit the far side of the base. "Soon," Bricker whispered. "So shut up."

17

Stepping through the doors of the Copper Queen in Bisbee was akin to walking through a door into another era. Everything from the bell desk to the striped wallpaper and whitewashed wainscoting led to the general feel and ambiance of a time long past. The hotel had existed for more than a hundred years, and the Italian decor looked a bit out of place to Bolan's well-traveled eye. This hadn't been built for the miners, but for rich investors looking for a comfortable place to stay while they played with their money.

Taking no chances, Merice and Bolan rented one room facing the street so they could take turns at watch. Bolan threw his bag on the bed and glanced at Merice. "I guess when we said one room, they thought that meant one bed." He shrugged. "If you want a different arrangement that's fine, but what I really want right now is a hot shower and some food. We can take turns sleeping and keeping watch."

"All fine with me," she said. "Why don't you see if you can dig up some food for us while I hit the shower?"

"Deal," he said.

THE ALARM ON Bolan's watch brought Merice upright. Bolan smiled at her from his position by the window as she pulled the sheet up around her and pushed her hair back.

"Morning."

"Is it? It still looks dark out to me. Can't I stay in bed ten more minutes?"

"I'd like to be across the border at first light."

"Okay."

Rough footsteps shuffling in the hallway had them each reaching for their guns. They lowered their weapons as the feet thumped past the room, fading, and Merice turned to him with a grin.

"That will always wake me up."

"Unknown feet outside your door? Yeah, better than any alarm clock."

"Back to work then?" she asked.

"Back to work."

SHOWERED AND SHAVED, Bolan slid his sunglasses on as they crossed the Mexican border on a small road that had been carved into the landscape by drug runners. Nadia punched in the coordinates that Tony sent them on the GPS and they maneuvered through the desert, keeping an extra eye open for problems.

They rolled the Conquest to a stop at the exact coordinates and jumped out of the vehicle. Tony stepped out of a crack in the cliff wall that looked like no more than a shadow. Bolan had to smile at the tracker who still knew his stuff.

"Good to see you haven't been killed, old man," Merice said.

"Old men are harder to kill," he said. "We're like leather. We may look cracked and broken, but chew on us and you'll find a hard meal."

"What's been going on at the compound?" Bolan asked.

"Sureno and his guys been getting busy in there. Looks like they're gearing up for World War III. No sign of your man, though."

"I suspect Bricker will be along anytime," Bolan said. "I don't want to hit them until they're all inside. If we strike before they get in, we'll lose some in the scramble. There aren't enough of us to get spread out too far."

"I agree," Merice said.

Bolan's phone rang, and he picked up when he saw it was Brognola. "Yeah."

"Striker, we've got a problem."

"Hal, if I had a nickel for every time you started a conversation that way, I'd be a rich man. What's up?"

"The ATF agents who were guarding Bricker's warehouse at Fort Huachuca last night were killed, and some weapons were taken."

"How many dead?" Bolan asked.

"Twelve at the warehouse, plus two more on the fence line, though that appears to have been a diversion," Brognola said.

"Damn," Bolan muttered. "What did they get away with?"

"Chemical weapons that were slated to go to another base. Sarin gas in small delivery packages. Bricker must have them, and as you know, he's coming your way. We're trying to work something out with the Mexican government."

"You know that's a political minefield. We'll never get the clearance in time."

"What do you propose?" Brognola asked. "We can't have cartels using sarin gas on anyone—especially not sarin gas that came from our Army."

"I propose that I get the weapons back before he can use them or sell them."

"Is there any chance of you doing this quietly?"

"Not much," Bolan said. "But we'll get it done."

BOLAN WATCHED BRICKER through the scope of the Tango 51 as the three-truck convoy approached the compound. The driving force behind this entire mess was in his crosshairs, and Bolan itched to pull the trigger but held himself back. The plan was a good one, and an early shot, however opportune, would ruin it. The caravan pulled into the hacienda and disappeared from sight behind the heavy front gates. Bolan signaled for Tony and Merice to shift to their positions. Until they moved in after dark, they needed to watch as much of the compound as the three of them could manage.

"Cooper, you there?" Merice's voice came through the small communications unit in his ear.

"Go ahead," he said, still peering through the scope. At the moment, there were few men and little action on the walls.

"Did you get eyes on Bricker?" she asked.

"I saw him," he said. "He was driving the second truck."

"Why didn't you take the shot? You could have ended a lot of this right there."

"Because taking out Bricker isn't the mission. He's

just the point man. The mission is getting the weapons back."

There was a long silence. "You weren't a little tempted?"

"I play for the long game, Agent Merice, and if you happen to get a shot before we go in, you don't take it unless I give the word. Clear?"

Another long pause, then a soft chuckle. "I agree you play for the long game," she said. "But as far as the mission goes, it's your call."

Tony's gruff voice broke in. "Aren't we supposed to be working here?"

"Roger, Tony. Merice, get to your position and tell me what you see when you get there. Tony, you all set?"

"Have been for two minutes now," he said. "Three guys just moved onto the eastern entrance, loaded for bear, and two more just joined the main-gate guard. Over the past couple of days, it's been one or two at the most, with a single rifle between them. These guys have assault rifles, sidearms and blades. It looks like everyone is preparing for a little action."

"Merice," Bolan said, "what do you have in the west?"

"Same scenario as Tony," she said. "These guys don't look like they want to welcome visitors anytime soon. I see some heavy artillery in two vehicles inside the yard and a couple missile launchers mounted on the back wall. Sort of makes me wonder who they're expecting at this party."

"I imagine a great deal of what we're seeing is for Bricker's benefit, as much as any external threat they might think is headed their way," Bolan said. "Chances are, the infighting between Sureno and Bricker is going to get ugly. In the meantime, we wait."

BRICKER STEPPED OUT of the truck and stretched his legs. The rough ride through the desert in the large trucks had been tiresome but necessary. Two of Sureno's thugs escorted him through the yard. Bricker noticed the increased presence of sentries and the disdainful expressions he was getting as they approached the main house. He could tell as well as anyone when a situation was ugly, and this felt like a five-day-old corpse in a swamp. He'd have to be very careful now.

They moved to the inner office, where Sureno was pouring tequila into shot glasses. Bricker couldn't help but notice that the armed guards remained by the door. Sureno set the bottle down, then slid one of the glasses across the desk as Bricker pulled out a chair and settled into the leather. He casually unclipped the snap on his shoulder holster while Sureno sipped thoughtfully.

"You've come at an interesting time, my friend," Sureno said. "Maybe a bad time."

Bricker shrugged and knocked back the shot. The burn was soft, almost delicate, the way a fine tequila should taste. "I wouldn't be here at all if you hadn't lost Stone and your men hadn't gotten so gung ho and brought the entire U.S. intelligence community down on us."

"Blame is a waste of time," Sureno said. "I don't think we should talk about blame because then I would have to bring up how sloppy you've become on your side of the border. I hear you've lost everything."

Bricker grinned. "Not quite everything," he said.

"No? So what is it you want from me then?"

"You want to be the big dog down here, and I want to help you *be* the big dog," he replied. "I didn't lose everything. You saw me come in with three trucks, and beyond the usual, I've got a special delivery that I think will interest you. It will make your bite a lot bigger than your bark."

"And in return for whatever this 'special' thing is?"

"In return, you keep me and my men off the radar for awhile. We'll hole up here and help fight off our mutual enemies, and when I get reestablished, you'll keep receiving your weapons. It's a win-win situation for us both."

Sureno swirled the last of the clear liquid around in his glass, then tossed the contents back. He stood and paced slowly around the desk.

Bricker began to sweat in spite of the air conditioning. If his plan didn't work out here, he'd have to go out into the Mexican desert. Things could get very ugly very fast in Mexico. "Maybe you don't grasp our situation here, amigo," he finally managed to snarl. "That Stone guy, or whatever the hell his name is, won't be waiting around. He'll come here, looking for us both, and he'll have plenty of backup."

"He's already here," Jesus chimed in as he stepped into the room. "He arrived before you did."

"What are you talking about?" Bricker asked, getting to his feet.

"I mean this compound is being watched. They've been staking us out for several days. We've seen their movements, but we do not fear what we know is already there."

"Then what the hell are you waiting for?" Bricker asked, exasperated. "Why not just take them out?"

"That's your problem," Sureno said. "You have no patience. The spider does not rush the flies into his web. He waits, and they come. Only then does he strike."

"So the flies are all here." Bricker gestured at Jesus. "You're the spider. Go eat them."

Jesus met his boss's gaze and raised an eyebrow.

"Bring them in," Sureno said. "Alive, if possible. Let's find out if it ends with Stone and his people, or if we have more of this mess to clean up."

They watched Jesus leave, and Bricker turned to Sureno.

"So you're in? We'll make a deal?"

"Let us see what the day brings, my friend," he said. "The spider is patient."

THE DAY WAS WEARING thin, and Bolan knew there wasn't much time before they had to make a move on Sureno's stronghold. He climbed into the truck and nodded to Merice as she and Tony joined him. They'd placed surveillance cameras around the compound for updates, but Bolan felt that they needed to change positions again. It was unlikely that Sureno was leaving the area unwatched.

"Anything else on satellite?" he asked Merice.

She turned the laptop monitor in his direction. "The new images are coming in now."

They watched as the resolution of the pictures slowly cleared. The trucks were spread throughout the hacienda and Bolan tried to reorient himself to the compound's layout. When he'd escaped, he'd been more concerned with speed than intelligence. Now, he could put the information from the satellite together with his own memories, which would give them an advantage, despite Sureno's extra firepower.

"What's that?" Merice asked, pointing to the edge of the screen.

Bolan studied the smudge carefully, then shook his head. "I don't know. Zoom back out and see if we can recapture it."

Nadia typed the commands into the keyboard and they watched as the main focus of the images moved from the inner sanctum of Sureno's compound to the base of the small mountain range to the south. As the image clarified, Bolan realized that it was another convoy of vehicles.

"Those can't be Bricker's," he said. "They'd be coming from the north. Tony?"

The camera tightened in as Tony peered over the console from the backseat to take a look. The old man made a tsk sound. "Not Bricker," he said. "And not Sureno. That's a new problem. Those trucks are coming from the southwest, and that whole valley belongs to the Cardenas Cartel. They must have decided that Sureno's good fortune in weapons needed to be shared. They're coming to level the place. Even with Sureno ramping up, Cardenas has twice the men that he does."

"So we'll sit tight while Cardenas takes out Sureno, then in the confusion we can sweep in and get the weapons," Merice said. "Simple."

"No, you don't understand," Tony replied. "Look closer. He's bringing in a lot of firepower, but that's only the beginning. If Cardenas gets in and seizes the weapons, there really will be no retrieving them. I guarantee he'll have more forces heading this way already."

"What do you suggest?" Bolan asked.

"You're not going to like it," Tony said.

"You think we should protect Sureno," he said.

"I think we need to get Cardenas to reevaluate his plan. Give him enough pause that he'll seek out reinforcements before they raid the compound. If we can get him to turn back, we'll take down Sureno and secure the weapons before he returns with his friends."

"That's a tall order," Merice said. "Even for a crew like ours."

"Yes, but it's possible," Bolan said.

"How? There are only the three of us."

"But Tony's right. We don't have to beat Cardenas's crew. We just have to make him think a little harder before carrying out his attack."

"I don't like it," she said. "It's got bad idea written all over it."

"Agreed," Bolan said, "but it's all we've got. Tony, what do you have for munitions?"

"I've got a small sampling. We can set up an ambush along Cardenas's route. A wash wide enough for our vehicles runs through there."

"That's perfect, but I want you to stay here and keep an eye on the compound. If they try to move out of there, you'll have to come up with another way to change their minds."

"Got it." Tony jumped out of the Conquest and grabbed supplies from his truck.

Bolan locked the truck into gear and drove into the wash Tony had pointed out on the map, maneuvering between large boulders and mesquite. The wash was wide but cluttered with brush and debris. The armored SUV rolled over the obstacles with little difficulty. He and Merice left the Conquest parked in the wash and climbed to the top of a small dune, scoping out their ambush corridor.

"We'll set up charges along the route here," Bolan said. "I've got extra fuel in a canister. With a small incendiary, that should be enough to send them home for backup," Nadia said.

"Then let's get to work," the Executioner replied. "I want to stay focused on those weapons."

18

Turning away from the monitors that showed a convoy of trucks headed their way, Sureno smiled serenely at Bricker's consternation.

"What do you mean, 'let them come?'" Bricker asked. "The Cardenas aren't small operators."

"This is a perfect example of why you ran into so much trouble north of the border," Sureno replied. "You panic too easily. You move before you think. Perhaps you have forgotten your training, or it was poor to begin with."

"I haven't forgotten anything," Bricker snapped. "Sometimes, you've got to *do* something to get something done."

"We won't need to do anything," he said. "Colonel Stone will do the work for us."

"Why would he do that?" Bricker asked. "He'd have to be crazy."

"You're thinking like a soldier, but consider Stone's mission. He wants the weapons and he wants us. The Cardenas will be an impediment to that. By waiting, we risk nothing and he risks everything."

Bricker nodded slowly. "I suppose that makes sense. The man obviously has a hero complex."

Sureno picked up the small radio on his desk. "Jesus, we've got company coming from the south. The Cardenas. Stand down and stay hidden until they're engaged, then capture whoever you can."

"Why not wait and take Stone's team all at once?" Bricker asked. "Maybe while they're engaged with the Cardenas? I could take my men out and—"

"*You* will do nothing," Sureno cut in. "Whoever we capture will serve as bait for the others. And that is how you kill a hero, you fool. With leverage, not brute force."

Seeing Bricker flush with a mix of anger and embarrassment was almost enough to mollify Sureno's intense desire to kill the man. For now.

THE CARDENAS CONVOY was six trucks long, made up of old M35 cargo trucks that were probably stolen from the Mexican army, judging by the remnants of the paint markings Bolan could see. The two-and-a-half ton rig was known as a deuce and a half when they were originally rolled out by the U.S. Army in the early fifties. The trucks were old, but they were easily repaired and could haul people, weapons and munitions over rough country with ease. Eventually, they'd been picked up by damn near every military, militia and warlord in the world for their general utility.

Bolan watched through field glasses as the convoy moved down the rutted excuse for a road that led to Sureno's compound. The trucks were too big to disguise, and the Cardenas weren't even bothering to hide their approach. Either Tony was right and they had backup coming, or they were packing a whole lot of heat in those deuces. Bolen hoped like hell it was overconfidence, or their whole plan could blow to pieces.

The last of the daylight was bleeding out of the sky in fans of purple, red, orange and gold, while the blue slowly faded to black. If they were going to force the Cardenas men to turn around, now was the time. Bolan keyed his comm unit. "Merice, go ahead with the signal," he said as he climbed out of the wash.

From the far end of the wash, near the road, he saw the flare streak up into the sky. "Done," she said as the lead truck hit its brakes.

"Second position," he replied. "Go now."

Through the glasses, he saw the M35s pause momentarily and then turn into the wash. Merice's movements would be nearly impossible to detect as the vehicles descended into the shadows that dominated the ground cover. So far, so good, Bolan thought. The trucks paused once again, and a squad of men jumped down from the back of the first deuce and started walking ahead of the slow-moving convoy. Despite their show of confidence, they were being cautious enough.

From his crouched position behind a cluster a rocks near the base of a mesquite tree, Bolan watched as Merice arrived at her second position, a cluster of scrub brush and more mesquite that looked like it had recently been visited by a herd of javelinas. They'd placed the charges deep in the wash and wanted the first half of the convoy fully engaged before they attacked. The men on the ground did nothing to change his plans because it was unlikely they'd see anything in the advancing darkness until it was too late.

"Standing by," Merice said over the comm unit.

Bolan put down the field glasses and switched to the Tango 51 again. It was crucial that they stop the lead driver. "Get ready," he said. "We'll go on my mark."

"Got it," she replied.

The M35s continued their slow forward crawl, and Bolan sighted the driver of the first truck through the scope. The low-light optic worked beautifully, so he could see that the man was leaning over the steering wheel, watching the soldiers in front of his vehicle like a hawk in case one of them should raise an alarm.

Bolan made a tiny adjustment for the angle of the shot, thankful that the wind had died down completely and that he had a good suppressor on the weapon.

"Mark," he said, gently squeezing the trigger. The .308 round pierced the windshield and hit the driver in the forehead, killing him instantly. His body jerked backward while his foot jammed down on the accelerator. The truck ran over two of the men in front of him before the others even knew to get out of the way. The wheel spun and the vehicle rammed sharply into the side of the wash, still accelerating as Merice used the radio to detonate the first of the charges, which hit the third truck in the convoy from both sides. The flying shrapnel flattened tires and tore through the camouflage tarp covering the back of the truck.

Even from his position, Bolan could hear men screaming in fear and pain. What was left of the ground squad hit the dirt as Nadia detonated the second package. This round of explosions took out the second truck. He saw the driver of that vehicle duck in time to avoid the first blast of shrapnel and glass. As he threw open his door to jump down, Bolan aimed the rifle, placing a shot in his chest and leaving the body hanging halfway out of the truck.

The remaining vehicles slammed on their brakes and began reversing through the wash, trying to escape what surely looked like a dirt alley of death. Engines revved and tires spun, kicking up a large cloud of dust. Cardenas's crew obviously hadn't expected explosions this far from Sureno's compound.

Flickers of fire lit the wash, and men were jumping free of the trucks, recognizing them for the death traps they were under these circumstances. Bolan sighted through the scope once more and found his target as a man tried to climb up over the side of the wash. The Executioner dropped him with a round through the heart. The cartel wasn't used to this kind of fighting, and the explosions had caused the panic he'd hoped for. "Last one?" Merice asked.

"Go," he said.

She detonated the last of the charges and the lead truck exploded from underneath as its gas tank went up in a giant fireball. Several men stood upright, coated in flames, and staggered away from the wreckage to die. The last three trucks in the convoy were out of the wash now, reversing down the road at full speed. The surviving men chased after them, screaming in Spanish. The Cardenas Cartel was used to being the powerhouse in the area, and they wouldn't have expected an ambush like this. Only other cartels would ever try to take them on, and then, rarely. Crippled as they were from Bolan's attack, it wasn't worth the hassle to stay and fight when they could retreat and come back better prepared. They knew Sureno wasn't going anywhere.

"Let's move out," Bolan said. "Sureno will have men here in short order, and they can deal with any survivors."

"On my way," Merice replied.

Bolan slipped the rifle over his shoulder and trotted

toward where they'd hidden the SUV. There was still a lot of work to be done, but for now all that mattered was that the Cardenas were out of the picture.

He slid into the driver's seat and waited in the growing darkness for Merice. She put her own rifle in the backseat, then climbed in. "That worked better than I thought it would," she said.

"They'll be back," he cautioned. "With more trucks, men and weapons than we can handle. And they'll be pissed. I'd rather be gone when they arrive."

"Agreed," she said.

"Let's check in with Tony and get going. The night's not getting any younger." Bolan clicked on his radio and keyed the tone that would cause Tony's radio to vibrate. There was no response.

"Try it again," Merice suggested.

Bolan went through the steps once more. Still no response.

"Is it broken?" Merice asked. "Maybe there's some kind of interference?"

Bolan stared through the windshield. "I don't think so," he said. "One more time." He pushed the button to toggle the vibration.

Finally, the mike keyed open. "They know we're here," Tony said. "Get out—"

The sound of gunshots filled Bolan's headset, then the mike went dead.

"Damn," Bolan said. "Merice, get that satellite feed back up. Let's see what we're dealing with."

Bolan put the SUV in gear and turned back in the direction of the compound. He had a bad feeling they'd be readjusting their plan for two people instead of three.

"Two trucks are at our last location near the compound," Merice told him, studying the satellite feed. "Some men are dragging Tony toward their vehicles."

"Then he's alive," Bolan said. "And he's tough. He'll hang in there."

"He'll hang in there for *awhile* maybe," Merice stressed, "but let's not fool around out here too long. I like that old man."

"Yeah," Bolan said, angling back toward the base of the mountains. "Me, too."

19

Bolan down-shifted the Conquest as the wheels dug into the sand dune, trying to find enough purchase to climb. The weight of the vehicle slowed their progress, and the tires began spinning in the sand without gripping. He hit the brakes, keeping the truck from sliding backward.

"Hold on a second," Merice said. She reached forward and flipped a switch on the dash.

Bolan felt the big vehicle sag slightly as the tire pressure dropped. It would give the wheels a larger contact area to grip. "Try it now," Merice said.

He was already in four-wheel drive, so he eased off the brakes and gave the engine some gas. The truck lurched forward. When the sand gave way to hard-packed dirt, Merice flipped the switch again, reinflating the tires. "It pays to read the manual," she said.

"So I've heard," he muttered as they crested the hill.

With so many people moving around the hacienda, the satellite feed could only provide limited help, so Bolan positioned the Conquest to overlook Sureno's compound. There was no guarantee they'd even be able to spot Tony; he could be in one of the holding cells or inside the main house. It was impossible to say.

Bolan climbed out of the SUV and trained his field

glasses on the stronghold. The walls themselves weren't lit, but the courtyard was brightly illuminated. Plenty of lights also were burning inside the main house.

Merice joined him. "Listen, Cooper. They know we're still out here and they know we're coming back. Maybe we should consider holding off until Brognola can send reinforcements. I had my doubts when there were three of us, but just you and I?" She shook her head. "It's a suicide mission, Cooper. You know it is."

He lowered the glasses. "It's only suicide if you die doing it," he quipped. "If we wait, Cardenas is going to return with more men and more firepower to take down Sureno. We can't hold off any longer. We need to get Tony and the weapons out before we have even more players on the field."

"What do you suggest we do?"

"I have an idea that might just get us out of here alive."

"All you've got is 'might?'" she asked.

"It's better than 'here goes nothing,'" he promised. "Get in the truck."

Sureno stood in front of the old man, who was tied securely to a chair. Bricker paced impatiently behind him, and when he tried to move closer, Sureno stuck out an arm and shook his head. "My house, my rules," he said. Bricker backed off.

"It's not too late, you know," the old man said.

"Too late for what?" Bricker asked.

"To get in your trucks and leave before he decides how he's going to kill all of you," the man replied. "I've known men like him my whole life. It's what he does."

Bricker paled slightly, but Sureno interrupted. "So you decided to get back in the game."

"I'm not in the game. I was just out hunting."

"Were I not your prey, I don't think I'd object quite so much to your 'hunting,'" Sureno replied.

"You're a small fish in this pond, Sureno. And you don't have to worry about us as much as the man standing behind you, asking for your protection."

"Why they hell can't you people just leave it alone?" Bricker shouted. "Lots of guys play both ends. Go fuck with someone else!"

"No one likes a traitor," the old man said softly. "And that's what you are, Bricker. A traitor." He cast his gaze at Sureno. "He tell you what we didn't get yet? What he's brought into your house?"

"Kill him right now," Bricker demanded.

"He's no use to you, Sureno. It's nice that he wants me dead, but you give him and the weapons up, and I'll convince the Americans to let *you* live."

"I haven't yet had the leisure to have my men search his vehicles," Sureno said. "What did he bring me?"

"A full Army Special Ops team if you don't get him and his weapons out of here," the old man said. "He stole sarin gas from Fort Huachuca, Sureno. You think the U.S. government isn't already making a deal with Mexico City to send in a whole group of people to gut this place and you along with it?"

"There's no army knocking at my door just yet, *señor*," Sureno said, his eyes narrowing. He turned to Bricker. "Is what he says true?"

Hesitating for a second, Bricker nodded. "Yeah, it's true. But so what? Those weapons, along with what I've already sold you, will make you the most powerful cartel in Mexico. The Americans won't risk coming here and creating an international mess."

"So you say," Sureno said. "What makes you think I'd agree to this deal, old man?"

"I don't lie, Sureno. The Americans won't stop until they have their weapons back. You have no use for this shithead traitor. At this point, he's a liability and he's going to get you killed."

"Shut up!" Bricker screamed.

Before any more words could be exchanged an explosion shook the ground beneath their feet. Shouts broke out across the compound and gunfire erupted in the night.

"Your man?" Sureno asked the old man.

"Maybe," he said, "or maybe that Special Ops team I mentioned. I guess negotiations are over." He shoved himself sideways, rocking the chair to the ground as bullets shattered the glass windows of Sureno's office.

"Mierda," Sureno muttered from where he'd hit the floor as he saw Bricker running out the door.

"You got that right," the old man said. "Waist deep and rising."

IN THE BRIEF seconds before the thirteen-thousand-pound weapon she was driving slammed into the gate of Sureno's compound, Merice experienced a brief flicker of doubt. It wasn't out of the realm of possibility that this maneuver would result in her death—and maybe Cooper and Tony's, too. Then the gates were in front of her and she braced herself for impact.

"But I always did like to make an entrance!" she said as the dry, heavy wood of the gate splintered, then shattered and fell. Despite her seat belt, Merice nearly slammed her face into the steering wheel. She floored the accelerator, charging into the courtyard and pinning two of Bricker's trucks in place.

Floodlights swerved to her position and shots sounded immediately, pinging off the Knight XV's bulletproof glass and armored body. Merice unbuckled herself, grabbed the remote fob, leaving the key itself in the ignition, and dove into the backseat. The gunfire continued, and the shouts of Sureno's men were closing in on her fast.

The back passenger door, closest to one of Sureno's trucks, was her escape route. She didn't need to open it all the way, just enough for her tiny frame to slip through. It was a tight fit, and the thick metal chafed at her jacket, scraping the skin beneath painfully, before she managed to get out, pulling her rifle behind her.

Merice shut the door, then hit the dirt, sliding under Bricker's truck then crawling forward. Sureno's men were still focused on the SUV, no doubt wondering why it was still parked there and still running. She could see their boots as they approached. When she reached the second of Bricker's trucks, she sped up and popped out from behind it like a rabbit out of a hat. Then she pushed the button on the key fob and the SUV exploded in a giant fireball.

The trucks shielded her from most of the blast, but the men closest to the Conquest had no cover at all and died, screaming and burning. Merice turned her attention to the inside of the compound and opened fire with the rifle, running along the wall to take advantage of the confusion. Her bullets sprayed across the main house, shattering glass and sending shards of adobe flying through the air.

Sureno's men were realizing that whoever had been in the truck was now loose in the compound, and she felt the bullets coming her way as she dodged into a small courtyard and vanished into the shadows. She was contemplating her next move when a slender hand reached out of the darkness and grabbed her arm. Before she could act, the woman spoke, sounding a bit winded.

"You'll die if you stay here," she said. She stepped closer, revealing an attractive, if bruised, face with dark eyes.

"I'll probably die if I don't," Merice replied. "Who are you?"

"Isabel," she said. Shouts echoed nearby. "I helped your friend when he was here."

"Let's go then," Merice said, eyebrows raised.

"This way," Isabel said, leading Merice to the far side of the courtyard. She slipped through the shadows with ease, indicating to Merice that she'd had some kind of official training.

They came to the wall of the main house, then the woman turned again, tracing a path alongside it. Behind them, Merice could hear men massing outside the entrance to the courtyard. She recognized the word for spotlight. "We're about out of time," she hissed.

"Here," Isabel said, stopping suddenly. She pushed on a section of the wall, which in turn spun on a silent pivot. "Quickly."

Merice followed her into a cramped, dim space and Isabel shut the door just as one of the spotlights flooded the courtyard. "Close," she whispered. "Where are we?"

"This passage leads right into the house," Isabel said. A string of tiny LED lights was hanging from the ceiling. "From here, it slopes down, then there is another door and we will be in the basement."

Merice considered carefully. By now, Cooper should have completed his part of the plan. She hadn't really expected to escape the courtyard so easily, but now that she had, she could adjust and lend Cooper a hand, instead of just acting as a distraction. "They brought a man in here earlier. His name is Tony. He's a friend. Did you see him?"

"Sí," Isabel said. "He was in Sureno's office when the explosion went off."

"Can you take me there?" Merice asked.

Isabel was silent for a moment. "He's probably dead," she said. "We would risk our lives for nothing."

"Friends are too rare in my line of work to leave them," Merice replied. "If you don't want to go, then give me directions."

"I'll take you," Isabel said. "If we're lucky, we won't find either Sureno or Jesus there. If that is the case, your friend may still be alive." She turned and headed down the tunnel.

Merice followed close behind. Above them, the house was silent, but she didn't expect it to remain that way for long. Cooper wasn't the kind of man who took on a mission like this and didn't leave a few bodies behind.

The least she could do was help.

20

Bolan moved from one desert shadow to another. With Sureno and Bricker both holed up in the compound and Tony now captured, he was out of time and options. The original plan had been for Tony and Merice to distract the guards on the walls while he slipped inside and took out the leaders. With Isabel's help and a position inside the compound, taking out the rest of the men shouldn't have been impossible. As usual, however, even the best-laid plans weren't worth much when the metal started flying. They'd patched together a new strategy, and all he could do now was hope like hell that Merice didn't get killed pulling off her part of it.

He reached the back wall of the compound and counted down in his head. She should be hitting the gate in about three...two.... He had just enough time to wonder if something else had gone wrong when he heard the Conquest smash into the front gates. Above him, guards shouted and scrambled in all directions. They were shooting already, which was a good sign. All the training in the world doesn't do much for a man who's been on pins and needles too long.

Bolan glanced up and saw the two guards who had been patrolling this section running toward the sound of the crash. He removed the line and grapple from inside his jacket, then sent it spinning in a tight circle. When he had enough force built up, he threw it upward. It cleared the top of the wall and he yanked on the rope, feeling the tines of the grapple bite into the adobe above him. He checked his weapons one last time, then started quickly up the wall. It wasn't particularly high—about twenty-five feet—and he reached the top in short order.

As he climbed onto the walkway, an explosion shattered the night, and Bolan grinned to himself. It had been Merice's idea to blow the gas tank using little more than a bit of wire, the heating element from the lighter and the remote starter fob. Still, it was a bit of a shame— that had been a very nice truck.

Bolan got to his feet and scanned the wall for the nearest stairway down to the ground level. He spotted it near the corner and headed in that direction, thankful that the two guards were still distracted by Merice's activity out front. Bolan reached them on cat's feet and drew the KA-BAR knife from its sheath as he closed in.

The first man he took from behind, cutting him across his throat and tossing him over the wall. The second man turned, surprise etched on his face. He tried to bring his gun up, but Bolan lashed out with a boot and knocked it away. Instead of continuing the fight, the man spun and sprinted toward the stairs.

"Damn it," Bolan cursed under his breath. The man began shouting for aid as he ran down the steps. Instead of giving chase, Bolan ran in the other direction, hoping to find a matching stairway in the opposite corner. He reached it just as the guard made it back to the top of the stairs with backup.

They opened fire, and Bolan heard the rounds striking the walls and walkway around him. He all but dove down the steps, taking them three at a time. His assailants lost the angle and the shots stopped as he made it to the ground level. He ran for the shadows of the main house, then pressed himself against the back wall, searching for the rear entrance he'd seen on the satellite feed.

He was almost to the door when it opened and Bricker stepped out, spotting Bolan immediately. He was carrying the standard Army-issue weapon, the Beretta M9, in his right hand.

"I figured it was you, Stone," he snarled. "Couldn't leave well enough alone, could you?"

"I hate to leave a job half-finished," Bolan replied, moving sideways into the gap between the back of the house and the outer wall. He eased off his jacket, revealing the holstered Desert Eagle. "How do you want to play this? Guns at ten paces?"

Bricker appeared to consider the comment, then shrugged. "Fuck that," he said, aiming the M9 at Bolan's chest. "I think I'll just kill you and go get a drink."

"Figured you for a coward," Bolan said, playing for time. Out of the corner of his eye, he saw that the guard and his new buddies on the wall were now peering down to the ground level, looking for him. "At least they'll know it." He nodded in the guards' direction.

Bricker fought the urge for a second, then risked the glance anyway. Bolan drew the Desert Eagle with lightning speed, rolled and came up firing, even as Bricker squeezed off two shots that went wide. The guards responded as Bolan expected, opening fire without being sure who was doing the shooting and forcing Bricker to throw himself toward the doorway.

Bolan fired again, his first round taking Bricker in the thigh and the second missing him by a razor's edge as the man fell back into the house, cursing at the pain and Sureno's guards.

The two guards were running toward them, and without a clear sight on either, Bolan held still, waiting for them to close in. Since Bricker's movement was the last they'd seen, their eyes were focused on the doorway rather than the shadows on the far side of it. That was the only opening the Executioner needed as he dropped the closest one with a chest shot that drove him off his feet. The other guard stopped with a near-comic expression on his face, but before he could raise his rifle, Bolan finished him as well. He edged forward to the door and paused, trying to hear over the gunfire from the far side of the compound. It sounded as though Merice was having a fine time of it.

Bolan peered cautiously through the doorway and saw that Bricker was gone. After a quick check to ensure that both guards were truly dead, he crept inside and closed the door behind him.

Ahead, on the left was an open door leading to a room with the lights on. Directly across from this was a shut door. Bolan knelt down to study the floor and saw the trail of blood Bricker was leaving behind. He'd obviously dragged himself a couple of yards, then managed to get to his feet, judging by the bloody handprint on the wall. The Desert Eagle was a powerful handgun and tended to leave large holes in people. Bricker must be bleeding badly.

Bolan watched the doors carefully for a full minute, and when nothing moved, he eased forward. It was impossible to know where Sureno, Jesus or Bricker were in the large house, let alone any of their men. Success in this kind of combat depended as much on patience and sharp reflexes as it did on aggression. To rush now would be unwise. Staying close to the left side of the hall, Bolan reached the open doorway and stopped yet again. Bricker's blood trail led into the room. Bolan paused to listen, and when he didn't hear anything, he went through the door, ducking low and scanning everywhere at once. He was in the kitchen, which was large enough to be a commercial operation. Sureno had men to feed.

Stainless steel countertops and hard tile floors combined with large refrigerators gave the space an antiseptic feeling. A line of ovens, grills and other cooking surfaces ran along the back wall of the house. The blood trail stopped a few feet inside the door, and from the look of the small pool, Bricker had paused long enough to tie off his wound in some fashion.

Bolan eased deeper into the kitchen. He spotted another doorway, leading—he supposed—into the rest of the house. Shelves of spices and baking supplies lined the walls, and on another wall, what appeared to be open pantries held yet more food. Bolan had moved forward between the ovens and the main counter almost ten feet when he heard a sound behind him and lunged to his right. Bricker's shot just missed his left shoulder. Bolan hit the stainless steel countertop and slid across it, coming down on the other side.

Damn it, he thought. Bricker must have backtracked to the other doorway.

"Come on, Stone," Bricker said. "Let's finish this like men."

Cabinets beneath the countertop prevented Bolan from pinpointing Bricker's precise location without standing. Thinking quickly, Bolan crawled back toward the kitchen entrance. Bricker fired again, the round pinging off the stainless steel surface then ricocheting away over his head.

Bolan reached the end of the counter and shoved the Desert Eagle overhead, firing twice in Bricker's general direction.

"Nowhere to run, Stone," the man said. "And nowhere to hide. You think Sureno will give me a bonus for bringing him your head?"

Bolan slid forward and popped out low, almost at Bricker's feet. He fired twice more. The first round took him in the crotch and Bricker screamed, dropping his bloody M9. The second round was more accurate and the lower half of his jaw disintegrated. Teeth, bone and blood splattered in all directions as the scream became a screech of agony.

Bricker went down as Bolan rose to his feet, kicking the M9 beneath the stoves.

The man was a mess. The earlier shot had taken him in the meat of his left thigh, which he'd tied off using his belt over the top of a kitchen rag, and the other two shots from the Desert Eagle had left him looking like a ragdoll. One hand clutched at his ruined manhood, the other at what was left of his face. He was dying fast, rolling back and forth in his final agony, one eye fixed on the man who'd killed him.

Standing over him, the Executioner said, "No bonus for you today, Bricker, but I get to put a down payment on a debt."

He was still alive enough, man enough, to know what was coming, and his eyes widened even as he tried to find his belt knife. Bolan shook his head at the vain attempts. "You're dead and you don't even know it," he said. He aimed the Desert Eagle at Bricker's forehead. "You're bleeding out, Bricker. It'll be slow. But I won't let that happen. This mercy round is from Colton Rivers."

He squeezed the trigger and it was done. Bricker had one spasmodic jerk left in his legs and fell still.

Spinning on his heel, Bolan turned and strode across the kitchen. It was time to find Sureno and put an end to this, once and for all.

21

The basement was little more than a concrete floor, three connected water heaters and a furnace that probably saw use once or twice a year in this part of the world. As the noise from outside died down, Merice realized that at least one of the problems with the plan she and Cooper had thrown together was that there was no way to know the other person's status without radio contact. They'd had to ditch their comms for fear Sureno's men would intercept their messages. For all she knew, Cooper hadn't gotten over the wall. Or he'd died trying. Or he'd died ten seconds after he got inside.

The other problem was that their separation limited the amount of damage they could each do in one area and made it more likely that one of Sureno's men might figure out what was going on. She felt the seconds ticking by and knew this had to be finished quickly.

"Where does that go?" she asked, pointing to a flight of wooden steps leading to a door.

"It opens into the foyer," she said. "In the back of the coat closet."

Merice took this in. Obviously, Sureno was more than just a tad paranoid—an annoying habit in a drug-dealing, weapon-smuggling thug. "Let's go," she said, starting up the stairs.

Isabel nodded and stayed close behind her. Merice paused to listen at the door before easing it open. As Isabel said, it opened into a long, narrow closet that was mostly empty and almost entirely dark. "How big is the foyer? Will we be seen?" she whispered.

"It's large," Isabel replied. "The front door is across from us. There are stairs going up to the second floor on both sides of the foyer. The dining room is to our right, the living room to the left, plus the main hallway that leads to the kitchen, the servants' quarters and Sureno's…interrogation room."

"Which way to his office?" she asked.

"Out the door, then left, through the living room is the fastest way from here," Isabel said.

Merice considered, then asked if there would be guards at the front door.

Isabel shook her head. "No, not usually. Sureno has had them outside, patrolling the grounds and the walls since Bricker arrived."

"Makes sense," she said.

She eased open the door a crack, thankful for the well-oiled hinges. A shout from outside the front door gave her a start, but the person moved on. She opened the door wide enough to slip through, and Isabel followed on her heels. Merice veered left and found herself in the comfortably furnished living room.

The room was decked out in white and brown leather furniture, traditional Mexican throw rugs and pottery from various regions—all of which was covered with twinkling shards of glass. Most of the windows were broken from the earlier panicked gunfire in the outer

courtyard. Now, with the exception of the occasional
barked order, silence ruled the night. What it really
meant was that she and Cooper were now being hunted.

On the far side of the room was a closed set of double doors. "Is the office through there?" she whispered.

"Yes," Isabel said. "Go quickly."

Merice crossed the room silently, then stopped short.
There was no opening the doors without being spotted by whoever might be in the office. She gestured
for Isabel to move behind her. "Stay here," she said,
then pushed the doors open, stepping back and waiting
for the sound of gunfire. When no shots rang out, she
headed inside.

Amid more broken windows, she noticed that the office led into the small courtyard she had crossed when
she'd hooked up with Isabel. Several overturned chairs
littered the floor and in one of them, she saw Tony. He
was tied to it, lying completely still, in front of the large
desk. Scanning the office for any hidden assailants, she
approached the older man and knelt down beside him,
removing the gag in his mouth.

He was breathing. "Tony," she whispered, shaking
his shoulder.

His eyes opened suddenly. "Nadia," he said. "Where
the hell is Cooper?"

She drew a thin blade from a hidden sheath inside
her shirt sleeve and went to work on the zip ties they'd
used to secure him to the chair. "I imagine he's around
here somewhere," she said. "Let's just get you up. Then
we'll find Cooper."

"Sounds like a—look out!"

Merice dove forward, but Tony's warning came a split
second too late and the blade tore through her shirt, tear-

ing the skin on her back. She continued the roll despite the pain, popping to her feet and spinning around. Before her, Kingston held a KA-BAR knife much like the one Cooper carried. Her blood dripped from the blade and she could feel it running down her back. She wondered how badly he'd cut her, then decided it wasn't important at the moment.

"Left you behind to guard him, did they?" she asked, adjusting her grip on her own blade and removing a second, matching one from her other sleeve. Gunshots would be sure to bring whatever guards were nearby on the double. "What makes you think they'll come back for you?"

Kingston laughed—a high, nervous sound that reminded her of a dying horse. "I don't think they will," he said. "So I have nothing to lose at this point." He lunged, almost tripping over the chair legs. Merice danced backward.

Some people were better suited for knife-fighting than others, and it was unfortunate that this was one area where her small size—and shorter reach—could be difficult to compensate for. Kingston closed once more, reversing his grip, then slashing upward. She blocked the cut with her left hand, darted in for a slash of her own and missed. Her short arms could be the death of her, she realized, skipping away again.

Her only advantage was her speed and agility—something the clumsy Kingston appeared to lack.

"Keep on running, Tinkerbell," he said. "Sooner or later, I'm going to gut you like a fish and your flying days will be over."

She caught a glimpse of a wide-eyed Isabel out of the corner of her eye and considered the possibilities. She didn't know for sure what kind of training the woman had, if any, or if she would act to help. Merice dodged Kingston's blade once more by darting behind the desk.

He followed, slashing sideways and catching her upper arm with the tip of the knife, drawing a pained hiss from her lips. "I can bleed you all night," he said. "You're already losing a lot of blood. Sleepy yet?"

Taking a risk, Merice went low and scored a slice of her own, the razor-sharp blade sliding through Kingston's pants and into the vulnerable skin above his knee. Kingston stumbled but stayed upright. He thrust the blade at eye level, nearly taking her ear off. She leapt backward, noting that Tony was still struggling with his bonds. Isabel had disappeared. The entire situation was getting ugly, fast. She needed to force Kingston into a mistake.

"Come on," she sneered, stopping her dance to taunt him. "You're as slow as molasses in winter. I can crawl faster."

His eyes narrowed and he lunged again, their blades ringing together as they each made a pass. Merice was tiring quickly as blood flowed from her back wound in a steady stream. She had to end this. She backed away a little more. "You fight like an old woman," she said. "Slow and sloppy."

He sliced the air, laughing his strange laugh.

She realized that she'd backed herself into the corner behind the desk. It was now or never time. "Don't need to hide," she said, straightening. She raised her hands. "I give up."

"You what?" he asked, stunned. He took a half-step toward her and she dove low, sliding between his legs on the slick tile floor.

With the blade in her right hand, she sliced his hamstring. She buried the other knife in his calf. Kingston screamed and toppled. She climbed back to her feet, knowing that she was about played out—at least until she could rest for a few minutes.

Kingston had somehow managed to hold onto his knife, and he turned around to face her. "I'll kill you," he said.

"Not today," she shot back, removing a throwing spike from her boot.

Growling, he tried to roll toward her. "I'll kill you! I'll kill you!"

"Oh, shut up," she said, whipping the spike underhand. It slammed into his throat and hung there, like some sort of weird new piercing.

His eyes widened and rolled back until all she could see were the whites and fell back, choking on his own blood.

"What an ass," she muttered, easing herself down next to Tony. "I'm bushed."

"Why'd you wait on the spike?" he asked.

"Forgot I had it," she admitted. "Mostly, I don't like knife fights."

Tony chuckled and shook his head. "Happens sometimes. Help me out of this chair. We'll get you patched up, then we'll go find Cooper. He's probably around here somewhere—just look for the trail of bodies."

Merice wearily got back to her feet, saw a pair of heavy-duty scissors on Sureno's desk and used them to free Tony from the zip ties. He rose slowly to his own feet, moving like a man his age—for once. "Uncomfortable down there," he said. "Now let's take a look at that cut."

Merice put the scissors back on the desk and eased her tattered shirt off her back.

Tony whistled under his breath. "That's a good one," he said. "It could use some stitching."

"No time for that right now," she replied. "Do what you can, then let's get going."

"I can help with that," Isabel said from the doorway.

"Where'd you run off to?" Merice asked without turning around. "A little help would've been nice."

"I was helping," she said, entering the office. "I shut off the security system."

"I meant with the dead guy over there," Merice retorted.

"You had it under control," she said. She opened a cabinet on the wall and pulled out several clean bar towels. "Besides, with the security system out of commission, we might have a shot at getting out of here."

"How's that?" Tony asked, taking the towels from her and opening the bottle of tequila on the desk.

"It's a centralized system—everything runs through it, including the radios and the cameras," she said. "Without it, Sureno is blind and deaf."

"That might be helpful," Tony said. He turned his attention to Merice. "This is probably going to sting a bit," he told her.

"Just get on with it," she said between gritted teeth.

He did, pouring the tequila over the wound. It felt like her entire back was on fire and she muffled her scream in the crook of her elbow. As soon as she'd relaxed a bit, Tony applied one of the towels to her back, then covered it with another. He tore the third into a long strip and used it to hold the makeshift bandage in place. When he was finished, he gently pulled her shirt back over her shoulders.

"That will have to do for now," he said.

"It will," she said. "Let's go get Cooper and finish this."

"Any ideas on where he might be?" Tony asked.

Gunfire erupted somewhere inside the house. "That sounds like it's coming from the kitchen," Isabel said.

"Then let's get cooking," Merice replied.

BOLAN HAD ALMOST reached the kitchen door when four of Bricker's men appeared in the opening. Bolan didn't hesitate, firing immediately while making a beeline for a large refrigerator. It was the best cover available.

The men returned fire, some vying to enter the kitchen and others attempting to back out, causing confusion. Surely trained soldiers should be familiar with indoor combat, Bolan thought. Not that he was complaining.

He peered around the fridge and spotted a pair of boots headed his way. He shot the toes out of the nearest one. The man howled, dropping his gun and hopping up and down—right into Bolan's line of fire. Another carefully placed round dropped him as his companions opened fire once more.

Bullets pinged off the fridge and Bolan knelt down, loading a new clip into his weapon. He leaned against the heavy appliance, reviewing his options. The fridge moved slightly under his weight. It was on wheels. Sometimes, Bolan thought to himself, the best defense was a good offense.

Bolan put the Desert Eagle back in the holster, then set his shoulder against the fridge and shoved, pushing off hard with his legs. The appliance moved slowly at first but gathered steam. Bricker's men had just enough time to ponder this development before he crashed into them with as much momentum as he could manage.

On impact, Bolan let go and threw himself sideways, drawing the Desert Eagle once more. The closest man wasn't able to get out of the way, but another did, tripping and falling. He clawed for his weapon, but wasn't anywhere near fast enough and Bolan gunned him down.

The refrigerator had rolled to a stop, effectively sealing the doorway, but on the other side, he could hear the two men pushing against it. There seemed little point in helping them, so he adjusted his position again, moving to the opposite side of the opening and waiting patiently for an arm to appear.

As soon as one did, he grabbed it, yanking hard and pulling the man it belonged to into the kitchen. A sharp twist reversed the elbow and Bolan broke it with a quick palm strike. The man squirmed in agony, and Bolan noticed that his nose was a broken mess—obviously, he'd tried to stop the heavy appliance with his face.

As Bolan shoved him backward into the narrow opening, he thought that the man's day was going downhill rapidly—especially when he caught a bullet from his own partner, who had fired blindly, stunned by Bolan's maneuvers into a knee-jerk response.

22

Merice and Tony took point, while Isabel trailed behind. As they passed through the foyer once more, Isabel directed them down the central hall. They turned and saw two figures struggling in the dim light coming from the kitchen doorway. Merice and Tony broke into a quick but quiet jog just as the light flared and a third man stepped into the fray.

After a series of quick, sharp grunts, the first two men went down in a jumbled heap. Merice and Tony reached the kitchen and saw that the third man was Cooper.

"Back in here," he said, retreating into the kitchen and gesturing for them to follow.

Once everyone was inside and Cooper saw Isabel, he smiled. "I wondered if you'd be around," he said.

"Yes, but I'm ready to leave," she said. "Sooner would be better than later, I think."

"Suit yourself, but we're not going anywhere until the job is done," he said, turning his attention to Merice and Tony. "What's your status?" he asked.

"I'll live," she said. "Just a good gash on my back. Kingston is dead."

"So is Bricker," Cooper replied. "I guess that leaves

us with only two—Sureno and Jesus. Where do you think they've holed up?"

"My guess is the courtyard," Tony said. "This is going badly, so they're likely to make a run for it."

"That makes sense to me," Cooper replied. "Merice, I want you to get Tony and Isabel out of here. Go to the rendezvous point and wait for our reinforcements." He glanced at his watch. "I imagine they'll be here in short order."

"Let Tony guide Isabel out," Merice said. "I'll stick with you until Sureno is taken down."

Cooper shook his head. "You're injured," he said. "And nowhere close to full strength. I won't have your death on my conscience."

She stared daggers at him. "I can handle myself, Cooper. Let's just finish the job."

"Your part of the job is finished, Merice," he said. "Now take Tony and Isabel and get to the rendezvous point. If you go out the back of the kitchen, you can cut left to the stairs and up onto the wall. I left the grappling hook in place. From there, it's a pretty short hike to where we left the rest of the gear."

She thought about objecting again but knew it would only irritate him further. "Fine," she said. She passed the Tango 51 rifle to Cooper, along with three more full clips. "You're going to need this more than I am. Let's get moving," she added to the others.

He slung the rifle over his shoulder, then grabbed her arm and pulled her in close to whisper in her ear. "Keep an eye on both of them, but especially Isabel. She claimed to be part of the Mexican government's organized crime unit, but something isn't quite right. She's not acting like an agent at all."

"Noted," Merice said. "Surprised you didn't mention her before."

"Slipped my mind," he said blandly, releasing her arm. "Get going."

She nodded and crossed the kitchen with Tony and Isabel in her wake. She paused long enough to look down at Bricker's dead body, then turned back to Cooper, who was watching them leave. "A little overkill, wouldn't you say?" she asked.

"Not at all," he replied. "Not even close."

She headed through the door. It would only take a few minutes to get Tony and Isabel over the wall, and from there, the old man could keep Isabel in check, leaving Merice free to return and help Cooper finish the job. She didn't like leaving a mission unfinished any more than he did.

GIVEN HOW MUCH time had passed, Bolan suspected that all of Sureno's men—and anyone who'd survived from Bricker's crew—would now be in the main courtyard. He heard no more sounds in the house, so once Nadia and the others were gone, he made his way to the front of the building. As he started to leave the shelter of the hallway and enter the foyer, he stopped short, noting that the front door was open a crack.

Jesus leaned casually against the far wall, his arms crossed over his chest. He motioned for Bolan to approach.

"Not the day you were planning, I expect," Bolan said, circling to his right.

The mercenary laughed softly. "Not quite. Even now, my employer is in the courtyard, packing up the last of Bricker's gifts and preparing to escape. I believed we might have as long as another day before you would attack."

"I'm known for doing the unexpected," Bolan replied. "I've heard of you, you know. Some of your work in Africa."

"There was good money to be made," Jesus admitted, sounding pleased. "And a reputation to establish. I see that it worked."

"You built your rep on killing unarmed women and children in villages," Bolan said. "Probably not what you dreamed about doing when you were a little boy."

"I was never a little boy," Jesus said. "In my country, few children get to be children. You're hardly one to talk, Colonel Stone. Your reputation precedes you as well."

"I don't kill civilians," he said, "let alone women and children."

"But you are not known for your mercy either. We are two sides of a coin, I think."

"If you want mercy, drop your weapons and surrender. I'll see that you get a fair trial."

Jesus threw back his head and laughed heartily. "Oh, my friend, you misunderstand me. We knew you were in the house. We assumed you would kill Bricker and Kingston, so Sureno sent me in here to ensure you were dead before we left. I have no interest in your mercy—just your blood."

"You're welcome to try to take some of it," Bolan said, "but you're in for disappointment."

"I was hoping you would say that," he said. "Shall we do it the old-fashioned way and fight like men?"

"Never thought you'd ask," Bolan replied. He took a step forward, but Jesus's grin and gaze over his right shoulder had him ducking and rolling. The pressure plate in the floor snapped and three crossbow bolts flew across the foyer, burrowing into the wall behind Bolan.

Not wanting to waste his opportunity, Jesus plunged forward, driving a shoulder into Bolan's midsection and knocking him to the floor. The Desert Eagle spun across the tiles. The mercenary landed a hard punch into Bolan's stomach, and his breath shot out of his lungs before he could bring in an arm to offer a block. He shoved upward, gaining a little distance, and blocked the next blow, then twisted, forcing Jesus off him.

Bolan followed through, whipping out a stiff arm that slammed into the other man's chest like a lead pipe. Now they were closer to even, both of them struggling for breath and trying to stand. It had been a while since Bolan had engaged in a good old-fashioned brawl, but some skills were like riding a bike, and hand-to-hand combat was one of them.

Jesus scrambled to his feet and staggered away, drawing a pistol from his belt. He turned and fired, but Bolan had already lunged to one side, sliding on the tiles and missing his own grab for the Desert Eagle. Somehow, he made it into the living room as two more shots followed close on his heels. One made stuffing fly as it smashed into a couch. The other round whizzed past his head with the angry, buzzing sound of a hornet.

The mercenary followed him into the dark living room, but by then, Bolan had his blade in one hand and a high-backed chair in the other. As Jesus began to move around the furniture, Bolan heaved the chair at his enemy, forcing him to duck. The Executioner charged forward, lashing out with his free hand and knocking Jesus's weapon away. The tiles were slick and it, too, skittered across the stone, ending up in the foyer.

Jesus wasted no time pining for the weapon as he tried a smooth roundhouse kick to the head. Bolan blocked, catching the leg in a lock and landing a punch directly in the man's groin. The muted howl of pain was satisfying, even as the bastard managed to twist free.

Bolan gave him the space, using patience as his weapon, as Jesus pulled his own knife and spun it in the dull light.

"I thought your reputation was perhaps exaggerated," he said. "I'm pleased to see I was wrong."

"Funny, I thought yours was, too," Bolan responded. "I'm happy to be right."

Bolan waited calmly as Jesus closed in, wielding the blade in a smooth figure eight designed to fool the eye as much as anything else. Bolan dodged the first attack. The second strike came closer, but Bolan blocked it with his own blade. Jesus tried again but to no avail. Bolan could see the frustration mounting on his face and waited for the next move.

WHATEVER WAS HAPPENING on the other side of the compound, it seemed to have drawn everyone in that direction. Merice set a quick pace along the wall, and she and the others encountered no guards beyond the two dead ones Cooper had left behind at the back door. They made it to the corner, and Merice gestured for Isabel to go up the stairs.

She caught Tony's eye as he started to follow and he paused long enough for her to point at Isabel then lay a finger alongside her own eye. He nodded in understanding and started up the steps behind her, with Merice bringing up the rear.

They reached the top of the wall and began making

their way along it, keeping an eye open for Cooper's grapple. When they found it, Merice said, "Okay, Tony, you're going down first. Then Isabel, then me."

"Shouldn't…" he started to ask, but she cut him off.

"I'll cover you from up here, and you cover me from down there. Isabel, all you have to do is hold on to the rope and slide down the wall. Just watch Tony and do what he does."

She nodded, not looking very enthusiastic at the prospect.

Tony checked to make sure the grapple was secure. When he was satisfied, he climbed over the edge of the wall and began lowering himself down, a few feet at a time.

Merice scanned the top of the wall once more and saw no one. Tony reached the ground and gestured for Isabel to follow. "Did you watch how he did it?" Nadia asked.

"Sí," she said. "I can do it." She grasped the rope in one hand and swung her legs out over the wall. Other than a brief moment when she slipped a foot or two, she made it down with ease.

Checking the wall once more and still finding it empty, Nadia leaned over to peer down at Tony. He stared up at her, shaking his head. Once again, she laid a finger next to her eye and pointed at Isabel. He nodded, then watched somberly as she cut the rope free from the grapple and let it fall down to his feet. Tony began to gather it up, and she worked the grapple itself free from the wall, then hooked it on one of her belt loops. One never knew when a spiky object would come in handy, and because she'd given Cooper the rifle, all she had now were her blades and one handgun.

She suspected she would need all the weapons she

could get. Glancing down at Tony one last time, she sent him a quick salute, which he returned, then she moved back toward the stairs. Somewhere on the other side of the compound, she'd find Sureno or Cooper or both. Either way, she was in this to the end.

23

Jesus was getting impatient and lunged forward. Bolan caught his arm in a reverse lock, then drove his knife deep into the soft spot below the ribs. Gasping, the mercenary dropped his own blade, trying to struggle free but failing.

"You… You bastard," he said, spitting blood.

"I've been called worse," the Executioner said. "By better men." He ripped the knife free and brought complete pressure onto the man's arm, snapping it at the elbow.

Jesus tried to scream but was unable to get a breath. Bolan knew his right lung would be rapidly filling with blood. The anger on the mercenary's face turned to horror as Bolan released his arm, and he tried to stagger away.

Bolan took out his knee from behind and Jesus collapsed on the floor, still struggling. He had had a lot of fight in him, but that was over now, too. Bolan knelt down beside him. "I know about you," he said. "I know all about the African villages where you let your men rape the women and kill them. I know about the one where they found over thirty dead children. It's over, Jesus. No one else will suffer because of you."

Bolan drove the KA-BAR knife into Jesus's neck and it went all the way through, erupting in a final gush of blood on the other side. Jesus sagged immediately. Bolan cleaned the blade before tucking the knife back into his boot, then retrieved his Desert Eagle. Outside, he heard the sound of several large engines starting and he knew that Sureno was about to make his move. He had to pin him down before he could leave the compound.

Bolan crossed to the front door, grabbed the rifle from where he'd set it down earlier and peered outside. Using a heavy chain, Sureno's men had dragged the charred wreckage of Merice's SUV away from the trucks, and the path out of the compound was now clear. He scanned the courtyard for Sureno himself but didn't see him. It was possible that he was already in one of the vehicles, but none of them had departed, so at least he was still in the area.

An adobe wall, perhaps three feet high, stood on each side of the steps leading into the main house, and Bolan took a position behind the one closest to the vehicles as he stepped outside. A quick scan revealed a total of four running trucks and about two dozen men milling in the courtyard, trying to organize themselves into vehicles. His best bet was to take targets of opportunity—starting with the trucks themselves.

He pulled the Tango 51 up to his shoulder and sighted on the lead vehicle's front right tire, squeezing off a round and blowing it out. The shot wasn't as quiet as he'd hoped—the baffles on the suppressor were rapidly wearing down—and Sureno's men looked around, trying to pinpoint the source of the bullet. While they were distracted with that, Bolan took out the front tire of the rearmost vehicle, boxing the other two in place to some degree.

The ping of rifle fire followed his shot almost immediately, and he knew that they'd spotted him. This wasn't an ideal location, but if it kept Sureno and the weapons from leaving, it would serve. Ignoring the scope, Bolan propped the rifle over the small barricade and squeezed off a handful of rounds. Men were shouting now and he recognized Sureno's voice over the din, shouting for them to kill him *muy rápido*.

Concentrated fire began on his position in earnest, and Bolan realized that he was pretty well pinned down. About a dozen men were firing at the top of the stairs and the doorway, not bothering to wait for their target, but just laying down enough rounds so that if he popped his head up, he'd be finished. His best cover was across a good twenty yards of open ground to the small sweat boxes Sureno used for holding prisoners. Twenty yards was a long way to run with a firing squad at your back.

Bolan was contemplating his best move when the shooting momentarily cut off, then resumed but in a new direction. Now they were firing back toward the courtyard on the far side of the house. Though he was unsure of who had attracted their attention, he took advantage of the brief opportunity and leapt to his feet, running as fast as he could for the sweat boxes.

"There he is, you fools!" Sureno shouted.

Bolan wished he had time to stop and sight the man, but he was entirely focused on reaching his cover. As he dove into the shadows around the sweat boxes, more shots sounded from the courtyard. Sureno's men didn't know where to concentrate their efforts. Whoever was shooting over there had effectively saved his bacon. He suspected Merice, rather than Tony, since she was temperamentally prone to having her way.

He paused briefly behind one of the wooden structures to reload, then he heard the sound he'd been waiting for—the distinctive *phip-phip-phip* of incoming choppers. He estimated three, and instead of bothering to look for them, he came back around the corner and took aim at the nearest of Sureno's men, dropping him with a clean shot, center mass.

As the helicopters got louder, he finally spotted Sureno himself, climbing into a truck. He tried a shot, but the angle was bad and the round skipped off the hood. The cartel boss shoved the big vehicle into gear and slammed forward into the disabled one in front of him.

Bolan moved back around the corner of the box. The choppers would be here any minute, but they'd likely only been authorized to do a strike on the compound itself. Bolan dropped the rifle and began to sprint along the wall as the first of the three choppers appeared overhead.

Running full tilt, he saw that they were Boeing AH-6s—special operations tactical choppers meant for ferrying up to five men into a difficult zone. The compound's spotlight swiveled around, trying to point one of them out and then extinguished as the troopers opened up on the light and its operator. The first one set down and the wind from the rotors, along with the covering fire, was enough for Sureno's men to run for it.

Now, all Bolan had to do was get to Sureno before he got away. Ahead, he saw that the truck was free of the temporary blockade he'd set up and headed for the remains of the front gate. Bolan put on an extra burst of speed and jumped, landing on the passenger side running board and holding onto the side mirror. Sureno saw him, swerved slightly, then pressed on.

Bolan tried to open the door as the deuce-and-a-half bounced down the pitted road, but he'd no sooner grabbed the handle than he noticed that Sureno was holding a pistol. He ducked down as the first round shattered the glass of the passenger side window.

"Hijo de puta!" Sureno yelled.

Bolan managed to hang on as the truck bounced over a series of deep potholes, then gripped the door handle once more. Another shot rang out as Sureno fought to steer the vehicle and shoot at him simultaneously. The truck veered to the right and caught the lip of the ditch, and Bolan felt the entire vehicle shake as the cartel runner tried to force it back onto the road.

Recognizing his chance, Bolan yanked open the door and dove inside the cab, chopping at Sureno's arm and forcing him to drop the pistol. Another punch landed on the man's jaw and the truck swerved back to the left. Elbows flew as they fought each other and the pitted road.

Finally, Sureno slammed on the brakes, shoved an elbow into Bolan's left eye and threw himself free of the cab. Shaking his head, Bolan felt the truck start moving again and managed to find the gear stick and drop the vehicle into neutral. The engine coughed several times, then stalled. As the deuce rolled to a halt, he jumped out and gave chase.

Sureno was running across the desert, not bothering to look back. Bolan took off after him, rapidly closing the distance. The man heard him coming, tossing a quick look over his shoulder and trying to find some extra speed. His physical condition didn't even come close to the Executioner's, however, and the gap between them narrowed even more.

When Sureno tried to leap over a cactus, he stumbled, missed and came down on top of it, yelling in pain as he fell to the ground on the far side. Bolan saw him go down, slowed and jogged around the spiny plant as Sureno was getting to his feet. In the moonlight, his eyes were wide and sweat stained his shirt. "Come on then, *cabrón*," he hissed, drawing a heavy combat knife from his belt. "If I do nothing else to pay you back, I'm going to cut you to ribbons."

He waved the knife back and forth wildly and Bolan could tell that he was no knife fighter. He should have taken lessons from Jesus along with his men, but like most drug and weapons dealers, he was more interested in money and hiring thugs than he was in getting his hands dirty. Sureno charged at him, but Bolan slid sideways, letting the man barrel past.

"You're slippery, Cooper, or whoever you are," he said, spinning back around. "I should have killed you on sight."

Bolan nodded. "Yeah, probably. You aren't the first man to make that mistake."

"I'm going to fix it now," he growled, darting in once more.

Again, Bolan stepped aside, this time adding a shove that sent Sureno sprawling. To his credit, he got back to his feet quickly. "Stand and fight, *cabrón*," he said.

"I'm right here waiting," the Executioner said.

Sureno came forward again, the knife held low. This time, Bolan stood his ground, dropping down and catching the man's wrist in his strong hands. He twisted and felt it crack as the knife hit the dirt. Yowling like a wounded animal, Sureno kicked and flailed, managing to get enough force into one blow to his cheek that Bolan released his hold and stepped away.

Cradling his broken wrist and panting heavily, Sureno stared hatefully at him. "Finish it, then," he said. "Finish it."

Bolan laughed softly. "It was finished the minute your man Jesus killed Colton Rivers."

"I'm not dead yet—"

In one smooth motion, Bolan drew the Desert Eagle and fired. The round took Sureno in the forehead, blowing the back of his skull off in a bloody spray of bone and brain matter. He tottered, then fell dead on the hard, unforgiving desert floor. "That's for Olivia and Katrina," Bolan said.

Bolan turned and headed back in the direction of the truck. Whatever weapons Bricker had inside of it, he wanted to make sure they were handed over to the proper authorities and not left here for the Cardenas to find. The worst of the night was over, he knew, but there was still road to be traveled ahead.

24

Bolan arrived back at the compound to find Tony and Merice standing near the gates. He pulled the deuce-and-a-half to a stop, shut down the engine and climbed out. The two moved closer, smiles lighting their faces. On the inside of the compound, he could see that the last of Bricker and Sureno's men were kneeling in a line in the middle of the courtyard, their hands and feet secured with zip ties. For a while, at least, this little stretch of desert would be safer for both the Border Patrol and civilians. That alone would have pleased Rivers immensely, Bolan knew.

"What happened to Sureno?" Merice asked.

"He paid his debt in full," Bolan said. "Though I think it was more expensive than what he had in mind. Was that you shooting from the courtyard earlier?"

"That was me," she said. "And unless I'm mistaken, I saved your ass." She broke into a laugh and Tony joined in, shaking his head ruefully.

"What happened to you?" he asked the old tracker, who was sporting the beginnings of a black eye.

"Isabel," he said. "She's not at all what she seems to be."

"What do you mean?" Bolan asked, concerned. "Where is she?"

"I took a call from Brognola a few minutes ago," Merice said. "Her name isn't Isabel and she doesn't work for the Mexican government. It's Ana-Maria Cardenas, and she's an operative for the cartel—specializing in setting up other cartels for a long, hard fall. The intelligence didn't come through on her until half an hour ago. She's practically a ghost."

"You've got to be kidding me," Bolan said, then turned to Tony. "And you let her get away?"

"I don't think 'let' is the proper word," Tony replied. "She did her best to coldcock me with a rock and ran off into the desert. I didn't feel up to chasing her at the time." He rubbed his cheek gingerly. "Still don't, for that matter, so find yourself someone else to hunt her down."

"Let her go, Cooper," Merice said.

"She's a threat, and she obviously knew a lot more than she let on," he said.

"Let her go," she repeated. "There's a nice little bonus here, if you do."

"What's that?" he asked.

"When she reports back to the Cardenas, Matt Cooper will be a name to fear down here, and so will Colonel Stone. Maybe it will keep them in check for a while."

Bolan thought about it, then shrugged. "Maybe," he said. "Or maybe it's time for a new name."

"Names are like hats. You wear the one that's appropriate."

"I try to," he said, "though I've been fond of Cooper for a long time now. Very well, I'll let her go."

"What comes next?" Tony asked.

"We clear the scene," Bolan said. "I'll need to call

Brognola, check in and arrange for all these weapons to be returned to the United States. I'm more than glad that someone else already known to the law enforcement community down here can help them with all the reports and paperwork." He shot a meaningful glance at Merice, who groaned.

"Come on, Cooper," she said. "You could help me with that stuff, too, you know."

"I could, but I have something else that needs doing."

"Oh?"

"I want to make sure that Colton Rivers gets the funeral he deserves and that his wife and daughter are doing okay."

"That is always the hard part of our world," Tony said. "It is not the names or the danger. It's that for us to act, often someone has to die, while the living must carry on."

"If it's all the same to you," Merice said, "I'll take choice number two every time."

"Better get that back-wound sewn up then," Tony said.

They moved into the compound and Merice handed Bolan his phone. "Thanks," he said. "And thanks for coming back. That was looking a little thin."

"Thin?" she said. "You're a master of understatement."

THE FUNERAL PROCESSION started at ten in the morning, and the sun was already riding bright in the sky. Bolan watched from inside the tinted windows of the family limousine as the honor guard led the way down the dusty streets of Douglas, Arizona, to Calvary Cemetery, where Colton Rivers would be laid to rest alongside his fellow officers who had given their lives to protect the border and keep the American people safe.

"What are you thinking about, Cooper?" Olivia asked.

She seemed to be on the mend, he thought. Her eyes were clear and calm, and Tony's wife was mothering her enough for any two women. A motorcycle passed on either side of the limo, the lights flickering and the chirp sirens on. "Change," he said, peering out the window once more.

"Tony told me that you were leaving today?" she asked.

He nodded. "Right after the service, once I make sure you and Katrina are home safe." From the seat next to her mother, the somber little girl looked at him but kept her silence. Since her father's death, she had spoken very little.

"And where will you go next?" Olivia asked.

They were at the gates of the cemetery now, and the black vehicle made a slow turn to enter. Behind them, dozens of vehicles—civilian and Border Patrol both—waited to follow them in. Colton's funeral would be very well attended, according him the respect he deserved for his sacrifice. For a long time, Bolan didn't respond, but as the limo pulled to a stop he realized that even without a new mission, he knew where he was going next.

"The future," he said, opening the door and then stepping out to hold it for Olivia and Katrina.

She looked at him with a curious expression and he smiled at her. "Tomorrow is another day," he said. "That's where I'm going next."

"And what will you do there?" she asked, her voice soft with the moment and the question.

"What I always do," he said. "It's what I do that counts, not the time or the place."

"I couldn't agree more." She took his hand. "Thank you—for everything."

The music from the honor guard lifted over the cemetery and he led the woman and little girl toward the gravesite, humbled to be among them, even for one day.

* * * * *

PAYBACK

A Mexican fiasco reveals treachery within the White House...

In Mexican cartel country to rescue an agent, Mack Bolan arrives to find the stronghold smoked and his man missing. It's the second failed play at the site, where five years earlier a mission went deadly sour. This time, Bolan suspects betrayal in the highest places. And when the mission shifts from rescue to revenge, the trail extends into the corridors of Washington, D.C. Bolan uncovers a wealthy industrialist with a rogue high-level CIA official in the game and ambitions to commandeer the U.S. presidency. It is up to the Executioner to take down this enemy of the state, and he won't stop until his job is done.

Available September wherever books and ebooks are sold.

GSB168

JAMES AXLER

DEATH LANDS®

BLOOD RED TIDE

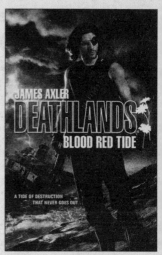

A tide of destruction that never goes out...

Taken captive on a ship in the former Caribbean, Ryan and his companions must work as part of the crew or perish at the hands of the captain. But the mutant in charge of the vessel is the least of their worries. Each day is a struggle for survival as they face rivalry among the sailors, violent attacks and deadly storms. Worse, a powerful enemy is hunting the ship to destroy everyone on board. Fighting for their lives and those of their shipmates, the companions find unity within the chaos. But in Deathlands, the good rarely lasts.

Available September wherever books and ebooks are sold.